The Perfect Woman

Also by Suzanne Harnois

L'Artiste inconnu. Nouvelles.
Montréal, Les Éditions Varia, 1999.

Suzanne Harnois

The Perfect Woman

Short Stories

Translated by Jonathan Kaplansky

VARIA
PRESS

Varia Press
P. O. Box 35040, RPO Fleury
Montreal (Quebec)
Canada H2C 3K4
Telephone: (514) 389-8448
Fax: (514) 389-0128
e-mail: info@varia.com
Varia Press Web Site: www.varia.com

Cataloguing data prior to publication (Canada):
Harnois, Suzanne
[Femme parfaite. English]
The perfect woman: short stories
Translation of: La femme parfaite
ISBN 2-922245-26-8

I. Kaplansky, Jonathan, 1960- . II Title. III. Title: Femme parfaite. English
PS8565.A639F4513 1999   C843'.54   C99-941618-9
PS9565.A639F4513 1999
PQ3919.2.H37F4513 1999

Varia Press gratefully acknowledges the
Canada Council for the Arts and the
Société de développement des
entreprises culturelles (SODEC)
for their support in
its publishing program.

Design and typesetting: Guy Verville
Author's photograph: Fritz Buchinger
Distributed by: Prologue inc.
Telephone: (450) 434-0306 / 1-800-363-2864
Fax: (450) 434-2627 / 1-800-361-8088

Legal Deposit: 4th quarter 1999
Bibliothèque nationale du Québec
National Library of Canada
Printed in Canada

For Ann, who read the manuscript
of this book twenty times
and for Fritz, who chose not to read it.

Contents

Translator's Note

The stories in this collection reflect Suzanne Harnois' imagination as well as life in contemporary Québec. Wherever possible, I have tried to preserve the "French flavour" of the text, leaving in expressions characteristic of the English sometimes used in Montreal, such as "autoroute" and "metro." I also leave in French the names of universities (Université de Montréal) and Cégeps, (colleges, equivalent to the two years following grade 11), and maintain the French names for streets in Montreal, such as Mont-Royal (instead of Mount Royal).

I hope you enjoy reading these stories as much as I did translating them.

Jonathan Kaplansky

Foreword

Each of the stories in this collection portrays different characters and situations. And yet, there is a link between them.

First of all, because the women whose stories I tell all long for a peaceful existence, and are capable of going to extremes to preserve this peace and equilibrium. That is the first theme of this collection.

The second theme is more general in nature. Every human being carries within him or her desires that are both secret and cherished. Yet in all lives moments occur when our own mysteries and those of the outside world converge, for better or for worse. The most significant, important events in our lives are the result of this irruption of dreams into reality.

Suzanne Harnois

Lady Seeks Young Wolf...

What could you infer about a clam from its shell alone?

STEPHEN JAY GOULD, *Wonderful Life.*

Men have always agreed wholeheartedly about the urgent need to satisfy their sexual instincts and their need for variety, for "young flesh," words which allow even the most colourless individual to identify with both Casanova and those terrifying cavemen.

No one, however, seems to address the problem of women who find themselves in the same situation. They eagerly marry an Adonis, as indefatigable as he is handsome, and barely have time to take advantage of the situation before he is transformed into an out-of-breath, fat, balding bourgeois, facing a mid-life crisis and completely inept at fulfilling his conjugal duties. Greek mythology is full of people transformed into trees, reeds or rocks, men who marry their mothers, or fanatics who burn their entire families, but says not a word about wives who are frustrated with their husbands. Another problem that interests no one.

This was a frequent topic of reflection for a woman

named Françoise, in the peaceful comfort of her beautiful home in a fashionable area, while her charming children were off at their excellent private school—and her successful husband Edmond was off somewhere in the city directing the business conglomerate that was his pride and joy. Françoise herself was in perfect harmony with this environment, which aggravated her problem, because she believed she had no cause for complaint, least of all about Edmond. The logical solution to her discontent was a discreet fling, but carrying it out posed serious strategic problems to a woman concerned about exposing her family to embarrassment. Besides, there was no obvious candidate among her acquaintances.

It was with the courage worthy of a kamikaze that Françoise sent the following ad to an alternative Montreal weekly newspaper:

"Lady seeks young wolf to make love with in the afternoon. 2345"

Françoise never doubted her ability to seduce a young man. Life had give her numerous opportunities to observe the power of her beauty, although she derived no vanity from this gift of destiny. Nevertheless, this affair would never have gone beyond fantasy if the devil hadn't gotten involved, which he did in the appearance of a charming literature student from the Université de Montréal, who sent Françoise the most disarming, innocent and inoffensive proposition to meet. When, completely terrified by her own audacity, she agreed to meet in a peaceful little café on Mackay Street, she found herself in the presence of a soft-spoken young man, lonely, far from his family (he came from Abitibi), graced with a mane of blonde hair, the most brilliant smile and a powerful, lean swimmer's build.

At the end of the semester, the student went back to Abitibi to spend the summer working as a lumberjack and Françoise decided to break it off. The student accepted this philosophically: he was a literary type. Later, he became a screenwriter and wrote a charming mini-series where he told of his early loves. It even won him a few prizes.

※❧

The next was a classic rocker type: ponytail, patched jeans, studded vest, and so on. He was a tender, sentimental lover who liked sad films and dimly lit bars, and who readily gave his mistress poetry anthologies. Françoise even accompanied him to a "Poetry Night." She spent unforgettable hours there, her head on the shoulder of the entranced rocker, listening to mediocre poets with no talent for delivery reveal their most intimate selves in public. This escapade gave her an intoxicating feeling of freedom. She had told Edmond she was going to Quebec City to attend a college reunion. He made his usual speech about how the upkeep of their house was costing him an arm and a leg and that it was always empty. But, as soon as he thought he had made his wife feel sufficiently guilty, he rushed off to rent a suite at the Hotel Xanadu, where he spent his night as a bachelor playing poker with some good-for-nothing acquaintances. He also managed to take advantage of the opportunity by drinking quite a lot of gin and eating all the unhealthy foods Françoise strove to deprive him of, as if he would drop dead by merely looking at a slice of sausage... He hoped she was having a good time at her reunion with all the old hens.

A few months later, the rocker found himself a job in Louisiana—in real life he was a radio technician. They said goodbye at the bus station. The rocker swore to her she had changed his life and that he'd never forget her. Then he disappeared, Greyhound-bound into the setting sun, like a true romantic hero.

The third was a man from the Far North, a prospector, who worked on contract for various mining companies and thought that job security in the south was for weaklings and women. He was a good-looking French Canadian: dark hair and eyes, stocky, very lively, and seemed to have emerged from one of the most turbulent episodes of our short history. He was stubborn, unpredictable and had a gentle way with women. Françoise and he got along very well, physically above all, but when he took off for new adventures, she was as relieved as she was sorry. This modern-day Radisson was sometimes difficult to handle, and, moreover, reminded her of Edmond at that age...

Françoise, who had become quite self-assured, arranged, in the usual way, to meet an Anglophone who
seemed to fit the bill. But while she waited for him in a
quiet cafe on Hutchison Street—where would we be
without cafés?—, she saw one of her husband's employees walk in and greet her eagerly: it was David
Moore, a YUPPIE administrator who managed one of
the business divisions. He immediately came over and
sat down at her table, grinning rather exaggeratedly,
she thought, for someone who had just met his boss'
wife. She took care of first things first.

— Really, David, it's a pleasure to see you, but...

— It's me you're waiting for, Françoise. I mean, your
date is with me.

A thunderbolt falling in the middle of the café,
between the sparkling Italian *expresso* machine and the
baskets of muffins, could not have caused greater con-
sternation. Seeing her panic, David took her hand
gently and said:

— Am I really more frightening than a stranger?
I love you. Speaking calmly, he continued.

He had seen her by chance, downtown, with a
young man. Small world; he knew the guy to look at. It
was the rocker who played in an amateur jazz band
with one of David's cousins. A birthday party one
evening at this cousin's place had provided a plausible
pretext for meeting and getting him to speak about the
mistress he had met through a classified ad.

— So, I looked for you everywhere, to see you again,
I contacted all the awful women who wanted to tell me
absolutely everything about their unhappiness or make

indecent proposals to me. But I never found you! I began to despair: I *had to* find you.

He could have phoned me, thought Françoise, her spirits starting to rise. She said nothing, however, she understood that all these complications were a result of his trusting nature, without which this date would never have happened.

This is how Françoise fell into bourgeois adultery. She never fully understood David's motivations in the affair, and he never explained them, even though confiding in each other was a key part of their relationship. In fact, his whole life he had wanted to do something forbidden, something secretive. As he had no leanings toward crime, and since hardly any other areas are off-limits in our permissive society, finding out about Françoise's secret life seemed to him a sign of destiny. He had finally found his heroine, his Anna Karenina and, as a result, felt as seductive as Count Vronsky (he'd always had a thing for Russian novels). But he could not tell her that the fact he was risking his job and perhaps his future by carrying on this affair— Edmond Falardeau was known to conduct vendettas— was precisely what prompted him to embark on it. Besides, he soon forgot about the risk and genuinely convinced himself he had acted under the spell of an all-consuming passion.

Everything continued along smoothly and Françoise wrapped herself up in the pleasure of the most decadent sentimentality. David sent her red roses. She wrote him very compromising letters, and the most idiotic love songs brought tears to her eyes.

One chilly spring morning, they agreed to meet at the café on Hutchison Street. They were sitting in front of their expressos, holding hands and telling each other sweet nothings, when Edmond suddenly appeared, and bellowing with rage, fired a hunting rifle at them.

At the trial, he in no way tried to deny his actions, freely admitted he had many faults, and had sorely neglected his pretty wife.

— But, he said, when I discovered she was cheating on me with one of my employees, I couldn't tolerate it: it was too ridiculous, too humiliating.

The Perfect Woman

*I never encountered a single interesting mind
that was not shamefully deficient.*

E. CIORAN, *De l'inconvénient d'être né.*

The Morins, Florence, Sylvie and Paul, were remarkable people who fully justified the most depressing theories on intelligence and heredity. Born into what can only be called an excellent family of good-looking, brilliant and nonchalant professionals, they had a lot of friends and championed worthy causes long before these became popular. The only thing that kept them from frightening perfection was that they were curiously inept at dealing with the prosaic details of existence. They were the kind of people who discover on January 1 that they don't have a rotisserie and go through life leaving behind them a trail of lost gloves, stray keys and unpaid parking tickets. Fortunately, finding an appropriate spouse can rectify this minor shortcoming. In this area, Paul had succeeded by far the best of the three. Louise, his wife, was very pretty and quite sedate. Slim, with beautiful eyes and long hair knotted in a French braid, she wore little black dresses and beige suits, and no one had ever seen her dress casually.

But above all, she ran her household perfectly; she was the kind of woman who is always on time, and never forgets birthdays, anniversaries, the dry cleaning, their savings-anything. And she performed these miracles daily, with good grace. She also had a job outside the house, in a translation agency-nothing that could reflect badly on her brilliant husband, a renowned mathematician and author of esoteric theories on the mathematics of chaos.

In fact, Paul would have preferred her to stay at home and take care of him, their two children and various related matters, but was careful not to mention such old-fashioned notions in public. Actually, he was forever praising Louise's many qualities: he had nick-named her the perfect woman. This chivalry didn't cost him much, because these were qualities he gladly left to others; he had better things to do. He never imagined that marital perfection did not come naturally to his wife: it was really the result of rigorous discipline and only by love, to ensure his pleasure and comfort in everything, had Louise taken control of the daily routine. This love seemed to him to be quite measured, like everything about her. He would not have burdened himself with one of those women who try to give them-selves completely, body and soul.

It was New Year's Eve. Louise was entertaining her sisters-in-law and their husbands, as well as a few of Paul's colleagues. They had drunk and eaten, and as their guests complimented him, Paul replied that as usual the credit should go to Louise.

—I don't even choose the wine, which is really a man's job. If it wasn't for her, you'd all be drinking plonk from the corner store.

—Because you would have simply forgotten, said Louise.

Her husband was standing behind her armchair and she lifted her head to smile at him. He smiled as well and wrapped his hand around his wife's long braid, a habit of his. She did her hair that way because he didn't like hair that was set or hairstyles you can look at but not touch.

—Yes of course, I would have forgotten, he said contentedly.

—So you do nothing here, just loaf around? asked his sister Florence, feigning indignation.

—I take out the garbage! But that's only because Louise doesn't want the neighbours to think I'm a wimp.

They all laughed and Louise smiled. It would have been less work for her to take out the garbage herself than to remind Paul to do it.

While Louise was serving the coffee, Paul went into his office for a minute. He was on the phone when she went to the kitchen, and smiled at her as she passed. On her way back, he hung up, and took the tray from her.

—It was that nice old Mr. Schusler, sending us his best wishes.

She accepted this, smiling. But her hearing was excellent. She knew the phone hadn't rung, that it wasn't a man who was speaking. It was a woman, and she knew which one.

When she had met Paul, he was going out with Sophie Deslauriers, a flamboyant slut, beautiful, heartless, depressed and with a drinking problem. This liaison, both exasperating and passionate, was the only one to penetrate Paul's perfect insouciance around women, if merely because of the terrible scenes Sophie created: jealousy, love, remorse, not counting the scenes that occurred on the spur of the moment, for no reason at all. But everything comes to an end. He was by nature too detached a man to put up with this carrying on indefinitely.

It was at this point that Louise managed to run into him often, as if by coincidence. Paul was captivated by her calm, gentle ways and her intelligent good looks. She was the kind of woman he liked. As for Louise, it took her years to recover from the inordinate effort this role of geisha cost her, seething inwardly with desire and jealousy all the while. But people get used to anything, and since Paul liked her like that...

Smiling, Louise served the coffee, and asked her husband no questions that evening, or on those that followed. She simply took stock of the situation. She didn't think Paul was seeing his old flame secretly. His busy schedule, and distaste for complication made this an unlikely scenario. On the last day of the year he had simply wanted to remember a woman who had certainly loved him. It wasn't serious.

The merciless mechanics that regulate the life of a perfect woman do not go off-track, get stuck, creak or protest. However, the ease with which he lied to her humiliated her intolerably.

One month later, Paul's secretary gave him a message from his wife, who asked him, without further explanation, to go pick up the children at the daycare. When he got home, intrigued and rather annoyed, he found a dark, empty house with no wife and no dinner waiting. Not a word of explanation, nothing, just a long strand of bronze-coloured hair on his pillow, coiled, snake-like. Fortunately, Louise had a brother in Africa. Paul told the children, who innocently believed him, that their mother had left for Tanzania to take care of their Uncle Roger who had contracted a terrible tropical illness.

In the days that followed, there were no signs of Louise. Paul, however, discovered that she had paid all outstanding bills, emptied the savings account and cashed in all certificates and investments. Then he understood that the trip to Tanzania would be a long one. His sisters commiserated with him, suitably enough. They would not have believed Louise capable of such a radical decision. But although they may have felt new-found admiration for their sister-in-law, from then on they looked circumspectly at their respective husbands.

After a few months of roaming, Louise settled in Florida, taking a job at the front desk of a large hotel. She took up with a local lawyer, who owned a travel agency, a sailing company and various other businesses. Belisario Alvaredo was overweight, forty-five, and looked older. He was a clever businessman, quite indulgent when it came to human weaknesses and without prejudice, financial or other. He provided Louise with an apartment on the ocean, a little red convertible and tasteless, very expensive jewellery. He always treated her affectionately, and when she got depressed, he promised he would go "collect" her children. He was not in the least bit offended when she refused his suggestion. He often took her with him on short trips, during which Louise came to realize that Belisario's business sometimes went beyond the confines of strict legality.

One day, coming back from the Cayman Islands where she had run some errands for Belisario, Louise was questioned by two agents from the Narcotics Bureau who responded cynically to her protestations of innocence and found a small flat package containing amphetamines in her carry-on bag.

The life and upbringing of a perfect woman in no way prepare her for such misfortune. But in this instance, Louise's panic helped her escape the worst. She protested, shaking, cried a lot and called Belisario to help her. It was nevertheless impossible to stop the trial. She also had to notify Paul, which threw her into a major panic.

Belisario met Paul when he arrived in Miami, greeting him like a relative with whom one shares a great sorrow and taking him out to eat out in one of his restaurants. There, over heaping platters of lobster, with long sighs and quite a bit of Chablis to drown their sadness, he told him the details of the affair. Paul listened, stupefied, as he spoke to him of his wife, now a stranger.

When Paul tried to see Louise, she stubbornly refused, in spite of Belisario's intervention. Paul was quite rightly offended. He had arrived in MiamI full of good intentions. Life as a single father and some disappointing affairs with people who tried to borrow his car or use him to obtain university positions had convinced him it was necessary to win back his legitimate wife. Most of all, he had no explanation for her departure. This complete and sudden loss of affection tormented him. How could a woman stop loving him, Paul Morin? It tormented him further when he realized he had been replaced by this overweight man, pleasant enough, of course, but rather common.

He was present at the opening of the trial, distraught and ready for the most dramatic theatrics (he occasionally read *Paris Match* at the dentist's, the sum total of his judicial experience). When the formalities were over, the prosecutor asked Louise what had brought her there. Her voice caught as she answered:

— It's my husband, sir. He was cheating on me.

The judge did not have time to explain to her that they weren't there for divorce proceedings, because Paul rose in the audience and shouted indignantly:

— Me! Never!

Astounded, he went on:

— With whom?

— With Sophie Deslauriers! You creep, look at where I am because of you!

— You're nuts! You're as crazy as your mother!

This reply was particularly absurd. Louise's mother was totally inoffensive and admired her son-in-law fervently. But Paul was so astounded, he could only reply with this familiar protest of wounded husbands.

— Don't you dare say a word against Mother!

With this, Louise sat down again and cried even harder; the judge pounded his hammer on the table, calling for an adjournment.

Paul, dumbfounded, left the room with Belisario, to whom he confided his clear conscience.

— I never cheated on her in my life! And with someone as hysterical as Sophie Deslauriers!

— I know, my friend, said Belisario in commiseration. The sad thing is, that's what she believes.

To tell the truth, Belisario knew nothing of the matter: Louise had never said anything of the kind. He believed, correctly, that Louise had come out with this outrageous remark in a burst of emotion, upon seeing again the man she'd left. He explained everything to Paul and implored him not to make any rash statements.

You see, my friend, she won't go back to Montreal with you; she feels too guilty. But we have to do something, if only because of the children. Besides, she's so nervous, she could never stand prison.

He naturally refrained from mentioning that he wanted to marry Louise himself. He was a man who clung to traditional values as long as they didn't conflict with business of course, and believed that a mother should live with her children.

When court resumed, Louise, clearly full of good will, said that the little package in her bag had been given to her by a Mr. Gomez or Lomez, a very polite man, claiming to be a friend of Belisario.

— I was quite embarrassed because it seemed this gentleman had already met me; I didn't recognize him, but Mr. Alvaredo knows so many people, and besides I was in a rush, so I took the package and said I'd give it to Mr. Alvaredo.

Belisario testified in turn. He claimed he didn't know any Gomez or Lomez in the Cayman Islands who could have sent him a package of amphetamines or anything else. However he implied that perhaps he had some unscrupulous enemies who would attempt to use a defenceless woman to harm him. Louise's lawyer insinuated that obviously the police had been tipped off by someone. In the end Louise was acquitted for lack of proof and listened to the judge's admonishments like a contrite little girl.

Belisario convinced her to meet her husband before he left. This meeting was not conclusive because Louise burst out crying again, repeating "Paul, oh

Paul" about fifty times, and didn't manage to say much else. Belisario saved the day once more by suggesting a very fair child custody arrangement. He then drove Paul, more mystified than ever, to the airport.

Louise and Belisario quietly got married a few months later. The children joined them in Florida for summer vacation. Louise was overjoyed at seeing them again. She explained to them she had met Belisario while taking care of her brother in Tanzania.

Paul, after some discreet mourning the ladies found rather intriguing, took up with a colleague he now intends to marry. His relationship with Louise is still rather tentative. He still can't understand... And yet, he gets along very well with his "brother-in-law," such an accommodating, understanding man!

The Lady and the Deer

*No man deserves to be praised for his goodness
if he does not possess the capacity for evil. Any
other goodness is usually merely laziness or a
lack of will.*

LA ROCHEFOUCAULD,
Réflexions ou sentences et maximes morales

The house was set up on a hill. From there it was possible to make out a few small clearings that vied with the forest and sections of the road that wound around the hills. In Lanaudière this meagre landscape can nevertheless be considered "a good view," as the area is singularly lacking in such vistas. But the forest, budding with the approach of spring, and the snow, still white, eased the solitude.

The small mountains and the narrow valleys of Lanaudière are home to several herds of Virginia stags, which everyone calls deer. The locals hunt them in fall and feed them in winter, in solidarity.

Danielle did this as well. Very early in the morning, and at dusk, she took the alfalfa Jean-Louis Michaud delivered to the end of the property. From the large living-room window she could see the deer come out of the woods for their food, but generally she preferred to stay outdoors. The animals were used to her. The sight of these gracious animals can alleviate any melancholy.

Yet Danielle could not be consoled, neither by the trusting deer nor the promise of spring in a pristine landscape.

She had just divorced. She was still living in fear.

Nothing, even her brief, disastrous marriage, could have prepared her for it. When Benoît realized that this woman, upon whom had gotten away with heaping lies and humiliation, was going to leave him, his anger knew no bounds. The trial was a long series of sordid slander, exaggerated recriminations and threats. Danielle, terror-stricken, agreed to everything, in spite of her lawyer's advice. All she wanted to do was leave and take refuge far from Benoît. When at last she ended up in her parents' cottage, she experienced a childlike feeling of security.

The shame came afterward, with the realization of her own weakness, her miserable abdication.

It was ten o'clock in the morning. Danielle had not yet fed the deer; she was waiting for Michaud, who was to have delivered fodder that morning. He arrived late, because a few bales of alfalfa had fallen off his truck when he had skidded at the bend in the road, below the cottage. They exchanged the usual comments on the poor condition of this portion of the road. The incline of the hill would have to be reduced, and the bend widened.

—At this time of the year, they should at least put down sand; the rest of the road is clear, but there's still black ice down there. I could have been killed earlier, said Michaud, a tad indecisively, as if this idea had just occurred to him, and not at all convinced of its validity.

— You're right.

— I hope you're careful when you come home.

— Oh, I don't go out much.

— You should, it would do you good. There's a concert tonight in Joliette, at the college chapel.

Michaud felt justified stating his opinion: he had always known Danielle. She was the daughter of a friend. He knew how much Gérard and Pauline worried about their daughter; while they understood her need for solitude after what she'd gone through, they didn't like leaving her there, in this isolated house. Later he would stop by their place and tell them she was doing quite well.

He said goodbye and left. He asked himself briefly why Danielle had married such an impossible man. His wife Noëlla, always well-informed about everyone, told horror stories about miserable Benoît. Since Jean-Louis himself had two daughters to marry, he did not believe that listening to such gossip was beneath him.

Danielle watched the truck drive off, then carried the alfalfa to beneath the shelter, except for the last bale which she took to the end of the field. She cut the bindings and began to scatter hay beneath the closest trees. She hadn't yet finished when the deer approached, showing their interest and impatience. As always,

Indra, the leader of the herd, walked in front.

Danielle had given her this name because of a Kipling story in which the Hindu gods, in the form of animals, hold a meeting. KalI was the tigress, Shiva, the bull, and Indra, the deer. Danielle borrowed a book on Hinduism at the library, where she learned that Indra was the god of thunderbolts and warriors. Although this association appeared incongruous to her, she still called the deer by the simple, sonorous name.

— Oh, you're hungry, I'm late...

She moved a few steps away and they began eating, stopping from time to time to look at her with their big, soft eyes. Danielle thought: "Only brown eyes look human, Benoît's eyes are grey, very pale, glacial, resembling an avenger in a popular novel, or a heartless villain." Suddenly she began to cry, standing in the snow, beneath the brilliant sun. Indra looked at her solemnly.

"I'm hopeless," thought Danielle. "Today I'm crying in front of a deer; soon I'll be taking Valium and telling my troubles to the closest listener."

She spent the rest of the day doing various small chores. Towards four o'clock, the phone rang.

— Hello! Danielle?

She did not answer immediately. Her heart beat loudly, and her vision blurred.

— Listen, sweetheart, there's no point in acting like you're not there, Benoît continued

urbanely. Where else would you be, if not at Mommy's and Daddy's?

— What do you want?

— I need the jeep. I'll come get it around six, six-thirty.

— It's my car, not...

— Your car, which I paid for with *my* money and I'm coming to get later. Bye.

He hung up. Danielle remained seated near the window, looking out, but not seeing. Why was she incapable, if not of resisting him, at least of answering him? What about this man still let him dominate her so easily? How could he continue to find reasons to despise her? Divorce hadn't changed a thing. She felt as if she carried her defeat inside her, like a physical defect. Even when they got engaged, she had thought she loved him and was scared of him. What a pathetic, ridiculous mess she had made these last years!

Daylight was fading. Danielle took her coat. She went to look for alfalfa beneath the shelter, but instead of going to the bottom of the field, she walked down toward the road. The bend in the road to the cottage was already filled with cold, blue darkness. She left the alfalfa at the edge of the ditch and inspected the area. There were still tracks from the Michaud's truck where it had skidded; very few people drove by here. A bit of the Alfalfa that Michaud had lost was still on the ground, perhaps about a half a bale. She removed her gloves to touch the black, shiny surface of the road. Undecided, she watched the narrow path made by the deer, first leading up to the road, then to the cottage. Benoît was a good driver; the kind of man who took himself for Gilles Villeneuve. But Danielle knew from experience that merely spotting an animal on the road would be enough to make him accelerate... If she hesitated, it was because the idea that an innocent animal could be the victim of this attempt seemed to her immoral. She lifted her eyes toward the clear sky, a silent, mineral blue, then shrugged her shoulders. She began to scatter the alfalfa, first on the sides of the road where the deer path ended and began again. After briefly thinking it over, she left the rest on the higher side of the bend, which could be seen upon reaching the hill. She picked up the binding that served to hold the bale together, and, even though she knew that not much time remained, forced herself to examine the area carefully. Everything was ready.

She practically ran back to the house, grabbed her purse and keys. She got in the jeep and started the engine. She took the curve gently, then headed towards Joliette, tires squealing.

She met almost no one on the road. She had a sandwich at a café in Joliette before going to the concert. A chamber music group was playing baroque music, which Danielle did not particularly like, finding it convoluted and not especially melodic, but that evening the formal music filled her with unexpected serenity. Everything seemed to her harmonious, reassuring: the overheated chapel filled with a golden light, the congregation sitting as if in meditation, the dark night behind the stained glass windows. During intermission, she met a school friend, Myriam Dubuc, with her husband. After the concert, she went to their place for a drink with some music-lovers. The conversation, on the merits of baroque music and the next summer's festival, went on and on. In the end, Danielle slept over.

॰॰◟

When she went home the next morning, she noticed, from two or three hills away, her father's red car parked in front of the cottage, and another car behind.

She did not dare stop at the bend, but slowed down as she passed it and noticed that very little alfalfa was left at the edge of the road...

Gérard had seen her coming as well. He tried to compose himself and thought for the hundredth time about what he should say. Danielle got out of the jeep, kissed him and asked him to what she owed the pleasure. At that moment, Gérard's companion appeared at the edge of the house. It was Paul Gagné, a local police officer.

— Did something happen?

— Yes... Where were you yesterday evening?

— In Joliette. First at a concert, then at Myriam Dubuc's, where I slept over.

Gérard and Paul looked at each other.

— Your husband was here last night...

— He's no longer my husband. Did he do something?

— Do you feed the deer, here? Gagné intervened.

— Yes...

All of a sudden she seemed very worried.

— Did Benoît kill one of them? I mean, Benoît's the type - if he saw a deer on the road, he wouldn't stop, quite the opposite. The deer have to cross the road to get here.

Gérard and Gagné seemed to be consulting each other again. Then Gagné said:

— From the tracks, that's what must have happened. But it wasn't a deer: he hit a tree.

There was a silence. Then Danielle said:

— He's dead?

— Yes. On contact.

Gérard studied his daughter's face, concerned. After all, this man had been her husband. What if she started to cry? He would not be able to console her. Pauline, her mother, should have come with him, but she had shown such ferocious joy when he had announced his ex-son-in-law's death that he hadn't dared bring her. Not with Paul Gagné in any case.

But Danielle didn't cry. She looked at her father and said in a little girl's voice:

— What should I do now, Daddy?

Gagné intervened again:

— Nothing, not a thing. We just wanted to let you know and find out if you'd seen anything last night.

— No but he phoned me in the afternoon. She hung her head, contrite. He wanted to take back the jeep, I knew it would only make more trouble, so I left.

— Well, said Gagné, now he won't make trouble for anyone any more!

Gérard kissed his daughter on her forehead.

— I must go, pussycat. Your mother will come up

and keep you company; she wanted to get some groceries before coming.

When she was alone, Danielle entered the house. In the kitchen she took all the bread that remained, carrots, apples and lettuce. She hesitated when she saw the sweet rolls, having read somewhere that refined sugar is very bad for animals. She put the provisions in a bag, went back out and took the alfalfa from beneath the shelter.

At the end of the field, she spread out her provisions on the ground and waited. Indra came out of the forest, followed by the others. As she didn't step back, the deer did not begin to eat and just looked at her. Danielle examined the deer with relief. None of them seemed injured.

— I am sorry about yesterday, I hope you weren't too scared... I brought you nice things to eat.

And she made a half-turn to go back to the house and wait for her mother.

Too Good to be True

We know nothing about the future, only that it will be different from the present.

Jorge Luis Borges, *Other Inquisitions*

—*N*o, ma'am, it's the starter, your car won't be ready 'till tomorrow afternoon.

The brakes were gone too and the transmission was in terrible shape. But seeing the young woman's tense face, the mechanic decided it wasn't the time to tell her.

—Oh no! The daycare closes at six!

—Do you want me to call a taxi? he asked gently.

—No, thank you.

Blushing, she turned around. He realized that she didn't have enough money to take a cab.

Behind her, Roger Wagnière, a regular customer, was paying for an oil change at the counter. He must have heard the end of the conversation, because, putting away his wallet, he said:

—Where are you headed? If it's in the same direction, I'd be happy to give you a lift.

The mechanic was glad that Roger asked this question before mentioning his destination.

—I'm going to Ville Émard.

—No problem, I'm going to LaSalle. If you're ready, we can leave.

Intense relief showed on the young woman's face.

— Oh, thank you!

Roger's car was a big tan-coloured Buick Regal.

— In my line of work a big car is a must, he said, as if apologizing.

— What do you do?

— I'm in real estate.

Like many of his colleagues, Roger had a knack for making small talk. And the young woman seemed calmer, now that she was sure she'd get there in time. He learned that her name was Sophie Desrosiers. She worked as a secretary, and had a three-year-old child named Éliane, or Lili. She did not speak of her husband except to confirm, in a flat, resigned voice, that he couldn't pick up the little girl.

The large car slid through traffic like a big gold-coloured fish. It was soundproof so that the stream of cars around it seemed to flow silently by. Sophie patted the velour seats contentedly, sighing:

— These large cars are comfortable.

— Yes, the sound system is good too. We're almost there—where is it exactly?

She wanted to protest, out of politeness, but didn't have the strength. She was so used to doing everything herself that she found the least bit of kindness disconcerting.

Roger watched her cross the street to the daycare centre. She was tall, and her lovely brown hair, held in place by a barrette, shone in the reflected light. The little girl was already dressed and Sophie held her up high, smiling, then rubbed her face against the smooth young face of the child. Roger had thought about taking her home afterwards, but when he saw her with the child he felt shy and left before they came out.

Bernard was already home when they returned. He listened to Sophie's plight indifferently. He had spent the day at the Artists' Council, now in upheaval due to the conniving manoeuvres of Perron, one of his close enemies. Bernard was distraught, complacently and gloomily holding forth on the effect it would have on the artistic community in general, and on himself in particular. He never let an opportunity to feel persecuted pass him by. After dinner he declared solemnly that he had to go out to tell certain people about the situation.

Sophie prepared dinner and listened indifferently. She only wondered why Bernard insisted upon coming up with such elaborate pretexts for going out, since he went out every night and she never tried to stop him. Or, more to the point, to go with him. Bernard's friends dismayed her: they were petty and self-centred. Somewhere, beneath all her worries and disappointment, she jealously held on to the last grain of idealism, her love of art. For a long time she hadn't dared expose this love to reality.

They had met at Art school. He wanted to become a painter; she was studying weaving. He had so impressed her then with his extremism, his anarchism, his theories on abstract art. Sophie, like many talented practicians, was almost incapable of abstract ideas. Her perception of the world around her was so clear and full that she didn't need theories for support. Yet then her simplicity had made her feel inferior and she provided a very good audience for Bernard. He was a rather puny-looking man with a scraggly beard, but even his ugliness seemed to her portentous. Later she was forced to admit that his theories were derivative, his anarchism an act and his diatribes on society merely the discordant rationalizations of someone who'd failed.

When she thought about this period of her life, it seemed to Sophie that they were both standing on a hill, holding hands. In the distance they were looking at a city full of towers, palaces and monuments, exotic and opulent like the Oriental cities you see in the movies. But when they entered the city the streets were dirty and dark, the palaces dilapidated and the inhabitants hostile, miserable.

After Lili was born, Sophie took a secretarial course and found a job. Just a temporary one. Although resigned to getting by on little for herself, she refused to let Lily become a Welfare child, and the loom began gathering dust in the basement. Bernard thought her decision to work was a painful one, of course, but necessary. When he went out for a beer with his colleagues, it was really quite touching the way he would deplore this sacrifice and the sad lot of women in the workforce.

Yet she didn't resent him. Why should he have to fit into a society that treated artists like dirt, and forced them to live in hardship, rejected them, underestimate their work? The only thing was it was she who had given up her dream, who spent her days in a window-less, airless corner, squeezed in between a filing cabinet and a computer. What really galled her was the way Bernard used feminist discourse to justify her support-ing them: he hadn't, however, acquired the necessary skills to do his share of chores around the house. So Sophie had to do them all. And even though women are compelled to devote themselves, she began to suspect that she had been taken for a ride.

When dinner was over, Bernard stayed just long enough to convince himself that he had fulfilled his family obligations, then disappeared. Sophie gave Lili her bath, then they settled in to watch a movie on underwater life in the Saint Laurence.

The apartment was small, a kitchen, a bathroom which seemed to have been added on as an afterthought, a bedroom, and a double living room. Lili slept in the bedroom, her parents in the second half of the living room, so they watched the movie sitting on the bed. Sophie took her daughter in her arms. She breathed in the sweet fragrance of her brown hair, while on screen watching schools of colourful little fish and undulating jellyfish. The whales reigned serenely in the gulf and a myriad of tiny creatures inhabited each wave. They had already seen the film countless times and each viewing evoked feelings of calm deep within her. It was the best time of the day, the time that made the rest worthwhile.

The following Saturday Sophie went to the shopping area not far from the apartment. She had to buy rubber boots for Lili, who naturally chose a horrendous shade of pink, decorated with dinosaurs.

Coming out of the store, Lili was jumping for joy on the sidewalk, displaying her new boots to everyone, when they ran into Roger Wagnière. He admired the boots enthusiastically, inquired about Sophie's car, then one thing led to another and he took them for doughnuts across the street. Sophie, who always felt shabbily dressed, noticed unresentfully that he was wearing a handsome tweed coat. He talked with Lili about life at the daycare centre, and Sophie asked him if he had children. He answered no, he had been a widower for eight years now. His wife had heart trouble; she died while out shopping. She was only twenty-six.

He seemed to be about thirty-five. He was of average height, stocky, with black hair. He had an expressive, animated face and people often asked him if he was Irish.

— After that, I was in mourning, and I don't know, I never met anyone else, I became a bachelor again.

There was a short silence, then they made small talk.

Three days later Sophie was leaving her office at noon. She had two hours of freedom ahead of her. She and her colleagues took turns having a longer lunch hour, to do some shopping. Sophie avoided stores as much as possible; they were a useless temptation. She had thought of eating a sandwich then going to the library, but ran into Roger on the sidewalk. Smiling, he greeted her and invited her to lunch at an Italian restaurant. He told her he was having a nearby duplex renovated before putting it back up for sale.

— If you'd like to take a look, it's close by, you could tell me what you think. Women have more of a knack for such things than men.

She agreed. Her sad little apartment frustrated her nesting instinct, and, like so many women in similar circumstances, she avidly read decorating magazines, picturing her dream house.

The duplex she looked at with Roger was a pretty townhouse, with stone corbelling, stained glass windows and high ceilings. With childlike joy she talked about ceramics, refinishing floors and insulation. Deep down she was amazed that a man was interested in these things, not realizing they hadn't met by chance. She had been inundated with work, worries and obligations for so long, that she had almost forgotten she was still a young woman.

After that she saw Roger quite frequently, but always in the most innocent of circumstances: he took her to see houses. Finally she realized that he was trying to please her, but he hadn't made any advances as such. She felt intimidated, held back by the same sense of duty that had pushed her into earning a living for her family, staying on uncomplainingly at a boring, poorly paid job.

But—ah yes!—destiny took over once again. The brakes of her car finally gave out one day in the middle of rush hour, at an intersection. She had fractured her ankle; a policeman drove her to the hospital. She was very scared and in pain, she was thinking of Lili. She tried unsuccessfully to reach Bernard and, all of a sudden, her nerves gave out. She phoned Roger and, crying, explained the situation as best she could.

He came immediately. He spoke to the nurses, turned on the charm and requested a private room for Sophie.

— But don't tell her it costs more, send me the bill, she needs to rest.

He blushed a bit saying it, and the nurses, suspecting a romance, purred their agreement.

He took care of having the car towed. He spoke to the agent in charge, informed the insurance company and Sophie's employer. Then he went to Sophie's mother, Fernande, to fill her in and ask her to take care of Lili. He brought her to the hospital and suggested going to pick up the child. Fernande was greatly interested by this story, but refrained from asking any difficult questions.

She had a strong personality and was not easy to fool. She couldn't stand her son-in-law, whom she saw as an irresponsible freeloader. But she knew that mothers inevitably win in the end. There always comes a moment when the daughter, embroiled in one of life's crises, lifts her eyes toward heaven and, hands on her hips, cries, "Mother was right!".

Fernande could feel victory at hand and was not about to ruin it by any unwanted gossipping. Besides, it made her heartsick to see Sophie raise her daughter in that rat trap.

However, when Roger told her he couldn't go with her to get Lili's things, because he didn't want to meet "him," Fernande looked sorry, as one must at such times. She informed him that this individual hadn't even married Sophie, hadn't even given his name to the child. She feared that her daughter, with her foolish pride, would not have revealed this crucial piece of information. Fernande had a profound respect for the institution of marriage, and thus had always thought it best that Sophie not have any sacred ties to this individual.

She was getting Lili's things when her son-in-law came home. When she told him about his wife's accident, he only managed to answer:

— What'll I do about dinner?

His mother-in-law looked at him disdainfully. She was slightly taller than him. She thought: "He isn't even good-looking. Sophie, my poor little fool, how did you get involved in this mess?"

Bernard realized his error and bravely assured her he'd manage on his own and would even go see Sophie in the hospital.

— Good, I should hope so.

— Fernande meant to say this ironically, but the effect was lost, as Bernard had never seen her not annoyed.

He went to the hospital, but the nurses informed him disparagingly that his wife was sleeping. So he went for a beer with his colleagues and made some

heartfelt remarks to them about how intolerably conde-
scending hospital employees were.

There were a few complications and Sophie
remained in the hospital for ten days. People were kind
to her and she found it very restful.

The day she was supposed to go home, Roger came
by around eleven o'clock.

— I understand you can go home today. He hesitated. I have something to show you, if you like, before
going home.

First he took her to lunch in an Italian restaurant
on the south shore. He spoke of one thing and another
with his usual ease. Then he took her to a new develop-
ment, an area still very wooded, south of Boucherville.

It was the beginning of June. The birches in the
clearing were raising their new foliage toward the brilliant sun. They surrounded a new Victorian-style house
with gingerbread trim, and an irregularly gabled roof.
Light flowed in through huge windows opening onto
the whispering forest. Sophie got out of the car,
hobbling on her crutches.

— Hansel and Gretel!

They went inside. The large empty bright rooms
resonated. Sophie waxed ecstatic while Roger praised
the house. They went out and sat on the steps. He told
her that the builder of the house had to move to
Ontario and that he had an option on it. Then, all of a
sudden, he blushed.

—You know, Sophie, if you like, Lili could go to school here. I'm sure you could find work in Boucherville. Or maybe you could take one of those rooms upstairs and bring in your loom. You could stop working, do what you like, rest.

There was an extraordinary silence, even the white birches seemed frozen against the sky. Sophie closed her eyes, felt weak, her head spinning. She realized that for the first time in her life dreams were coming true. An ordinary man had turned into a prince, and was offering her love, security and a castle in the forest.

Autoroute

Only their love matters to me. It doesn't inter-
est me because it moves or surprises me, or
makes me dream, but because it brings to mind
a youthful memory, a strange memory of a
hunt where love appeared to me, the way
crosses in the sky appeared to the first Chris-
tians.

GUY DE MAUPASSANT, *Amour*

Even in death, the young man was very handsome. To an objective onlooker, the bleak lighting of the morgue and terrible beating he had taken only made his beauty pathetic: a mutilated masterpiece. When his wife came to identify him, accompanied by her sister and Inspector Pelchat, she gently touched the side of his face that remained intact, and murmured: "François, François... " Only when she was outside did she begin to cry uncontrollably.

The crime had been committed at a rest area on Highway 20. The victim, returning from Quebec City, had stopped, it seemed, to relieve himself. There he was approached and attacked by one or more individuals. The police knew the rest area was a meeting ground for male prostitutes and their customers. Lately, however, it was also a hunting ground for gangs of skinheads, who got their kicks by fag bashing. None of their victims had ever complained...

Inspector Pelchat attended François Fortier's

funeral, not so much to find suspects as to talk to friends and relatives of the deceased. These conversations confirmed his suspicions: François Fortier had just stopped there by coincidence, and his murder was a mistake.

The inspector had no choice but to discuss this theory with the wife of the deceased. Julie listened incredulously, then burst into tears. Her sister Adrienne answered for her, resentfully, as if Pelchat had come up with this outrageous theory only to further distress Julie.

— If you know that, why don't you arrest these skinheads?

— Because there's no proof... Not yet...

Adrienne replied that, in that case, it was pointless to come here with such sordid details and that they'd had quite enough for today.

At the burial, the young widow seemed so broken up that people kindly refrained from murmuring the usual platitudes. It's hard to say that a man killed in the prime of life looks as if he's asleep or that it's all for the best. But life goes on, and after many tears, the funeral-goers went home and Julie found herself alone.

When the police told her about the disaster, Julie found herself unable to believe it. But since then, she had discovered that it was the most believable thing in the world. She was reminded of François' death continually; its reality hit her in the face each moment of the day and night. She hadn't gone back to her job as a dietician. During the day she knocked herself out doing chores, but the nights and mornings were unbearable.

François had been in the habit of getting up early. He would drink his coffee standing up, looking out the window. Julie, laughing, called this stance atavistic: he resembled a prehistoric hunter surveying his territory from the entrance of his cave, in LaSalle. She had gazed at him with satisfaction every morning, admiring his dark hair, long muscular neck, the harmonious movements that flowed like a series of invisible curves in the air, a beauty as familiar as the sunrise. It belonged to her alone: the exquisite scent of his skin, the perfect rhythm of his body, the moment he was in her like a river flowing into the sea...

And all this had ended, in the most brutal, sordid way possible. She wrung her hands in sorrow and regret, and turned around in circles, wailing, persuaded she would die just as surely as people die of hunger.

Her misfortune had turned her into an insomniac; she spent the darkest part of her nights drinking cognac and smoking. Sometimes, when the tension became intolerable, she would get in the car the police had brought back and drive around aimlessly, while the radio blared out incomprehensible, obsessive rock tunes.

At first she headed downtown because the lights and heavy traffic provided a diversion from her torment. But she almost had an accident at the corner of Saint-Denis and Mont-Royal. She knew then she was driving "under the influence" and that it was unfair to assume that everyone else was as sick of life as she. She changed her itinerary, first driving around the expressways surrounding Montreal, then, as the outings became longer, heading towards the suburbs, then the autoroutes. After driving for hours at night, she would sometimes stop in a restaurant for a cup of coffee and maybe something to eat. Sitting alone among strangers who were just as tired as she, she felt an uncertain peace, and her suffering disappeared, the way it does when a patient is heavily sedated after a serious operation.

As she continued to roam, she inevitably ended up on the 20, near 'the' rest stop.

She passed by it several times without stopping: just being near this place terrified her, even through her frozen cocoon. But she hardened herself and one night she dared stop. She parked in a dark spot near the end of the parking lot. Near a small hut, a group of young men stood laughing and smoking, their shaved heads shiny beneath the street lamp.

She hurriedly got back into her car and started it, as if having witnessed something obscene. She was flushed and her eyes filled with tears. Everything the inspector had said was true, then: François was dead, and she was only half alive, a dark presence forever at her side. But, for his killers, nothing had changed. She spent the rest of the night driving around Montreal in frenzied distress, not returning home until dawn.

But she was drawn back to the autoroute. Powerless to resist, she returned again and again, to watch them.

※ℒ

Sometimes different men, looking both arrogant and stealthy, were there as well. Sometimes the police remained parked in the area for hours, and everyone stared at each other like statues. The comings and goings of the various groups seemed to be ruled by mysterious rhythms, like the movements of flocks of animals. She would have to be very patient in order to find out what she needed to know...

She returned one cold rainy night, when the autoroute was practically deserted. Like the first time, she parked her car far off, in the shadows. She drew in her raincoat tightly and headed towards the wash-rooms.

This small structure was divided into two parts, one for men, the other for women. The gang stayed on the men's side and whistled at her halfheartedly: she was too far away for them to see whether her face was young or old. The one she knew to be their leader, bigger and stronger than the others, was standing guard alone, as befits a leader.

When she passed close to him, he had just lit a cigarette. She hesitated, and, lowering her head, stepped aside. He smiled slowly, self-importantly, for he had noticed her fear. When she entered the structure, he took another drag or two of his cigarette. Then he ground it out under his boot and entered the women's washroom. As soon as he walked in, Julie, who had crouched behind the door, hit him in the temple with the tire jack hidden inside her raincoat. She swung with all her might, and he fell forward in a heap. She pushed him rapidly beneath the counter, where he was partially hidden by the door. She went out and got back into her car, without passing too closely to the others. She drove for a long time, not thinking of anything. When she finally got home, she slept like a log.

Soon after, Inspector Pelchat came to see her. She offered him a cup of coffee and they sat in the kitchen.

— Did you see the newspaper?

— Yes...

— More news this morning. A friend of Pednault, the guy who was murdered, came to see us with his father. He told us that Pednault...—he paused for a minute—killed your husband.

As she looked at him without saying anything, he continued. They always operated in the same way. One of them came on to the homosexuals who hang out in the area. He would lead him off somewhere, then signal the others, who would beat him up.

— The guy said it was Pednault who made advances to your husband, that your husband told him to get lost and Pednault had a fit... it went too far... Afterwards Pednault threatened them, and since they were accomplices, after all, they kept quiet.

Julie gripped the side of the table and said in a tense, sarcastic voice:

— It's all rather convenient, eh? This guy, Pednault, gets killed and he's the murderer? It's really quite convenient. Who killed him? Do you know?

— No, the others say they saw nothing...

— Maybe they did it...

— I don't think so. We picked up the rest of the gang-they're scared stiff... Your husband wasn't their only victim. The others didn't complain—that doesn't mean that they didn't want to take revenge. And, you know, that guy was a real good-for-nothing, he had already been in trouble with us: assault, theft, vandalism. We can't prove anything without the testimony from the others, but I think it's true. We already interrogated them separately. The testimonies match.

There was a silence. Julie had tears in her eyes. The inspector said softly:

— I know it's not my business ma'am, but it might be better if you left this place. I know you can't ever forget this, but it really would help you to move, find another job. If you stay here, you'll always to be thinking of him.

— Yes, I'm sure you're right.

Julie sold the house to the first buyer who made a reasonable offer. She found a job in a clinic in the Maritimes, in Acadia, right by the ocean. The newspapers said that the trial of the skinheads was progressing.

They had not found Pednault's attacker. She sold the car to a couple of young German tourists who wanted to drive out west, and bought herself a new car.

The day before she left, she cut all the flowers in the garden. Peonies were in bloom. The car was filled with their sensual aroma as she drove to the Mont-Royal cemetery. She carried armfuls of peonies to François' grave. She had not brought water or a vase: they would wilt rapidly in the heat, but perhaps that was best, as she had brought them as a gesture of fare-well. She looked at the calm, green cemetery, unper-turbed by the city's muffled roar that sounded like surf lapping up against a peaceful island, and knew that it was finally all over.

The Friend

*No man will ever know the exact truth of this
story; though women may sometimes whisper
it to one another after a dance, when they are
putting up their hair for the night and compar-
ing lists of victims.*

RUDYARD KIPLING, *False Dawn*

Julienne's and Elizabeth's mothers
had known each other since elementary school and had
been friends all their lives. They had gotten married at
the same age and had little girls at the same time, so it
was natural that this exemplary friendship be passed on
to their children. Now in their mid-thirties, Julienne
and Elizabeth were like sisters-even more than sisters:
they had chosen each other.

Julienne had gotten married twelve years earlier to
Gérard Dubuc, an assistant manager at Talleyrand and
Associates, a machine tool company. He was a good-
looking man, tall, broad-shouldered, blond, good-
natured, quite sociable and steadfast, and a sharp businessman. He was a bit fat, but carried his weight easily,
as somehow additional proof of his success. He was
quite the opposite of a faithful husband. Yet he was careful, because he thought the rights of his legitimate and
irreproachable spouse, mother of his children, were
inalienable, and that divorce was a disgrace, really, alto-

gether unworthy of a responsible man.

Elizabeth did not enjoy such a stable emotional climate. Seven years earlier, she had worked as a chartered accountant for a well-known firm where, showing a great deal of flare and earning large profits, she was the "token woman." She lived practically, like women who have truly acquired independence.

For her sins, she became involved with a man named Roch Marquis, whom she had met at the Montreal Pool Room, going there one night with a gang of friends to eat steamed hot dogs. He taught her to play pool, flirted with her outrageously and showered her with extravagant compliments. He was good-looking as well, with the unlikely air of a South American seducer. Would Elizabeth have been as naive had she not always lived and worked in a milieu where sexual harassment was a deadly sin? Was it simply biological fate at its worst? Whatever the case, she fell into his arms, as if falling down a flight of stairs. She believed everything he said, did everything he wanted, lent him her apartment, her car, her credit card. She introduced him to Julienne and her husband. Julienne thought he was the kind of man who makes you want to count the silver and refrained from commenting.

It all ended very badly, of course. Roch Marquis was arrested for forgery, using forged currency, fraud, embezzlement, blackmail, and so on. Elizabeth was floored: she took it very hard, and her professional competence made such naivete seem suspicious. A trial was held and she was formally cleared.

Unfortunately, at the time of the trial, the fine city

of Montreal was singularly lacking in scandal, and the tabloids threw themselves like vultures onto the Marquis affair. Elizabeth was portrayed in turn as a shady businesswoman, an imbecile, a professional who liked slumming, and a nymphomaniac who kept an army of gigolos. She hit rock bottom when Marquis' legitimate wife appeared on the scene.

Ginette Marquis was a tearful, idiotic creature, who arrived in court flanked by two snotty little brats and an assistant social worker. She understood nothing of what the judge told her, but with the help of the social worker managed to testify that her husband had left her again, this time for an accountant, that he only came to see her to take away her social assistance cheque and slap her around, "and, while we're here, if your Honour would be so kind as to grant a divorce, because she's had enough." Poor Ginette did not get her divorce, not immediately, anyway, and the most obvious outcome of the matter was that Elizabeth now found herself being accused of bigamy, abusing widows and orphans, and embezzling Welfare funds.

At the beginning of the trial, she had moved in with Julienne to escape her tormentors, the journalists. That evening, she threw herself into her friend's arms, crying in rage and humiliation. Julienne patted her on the back, gave her a large whisky and asked no questions. She did the same thing throughout the trial. Not only did she ask nothing of Elizabeth, she didn't read any accounts of the trial, and never went to the court house. She showed the most supreme indifference to the countless people she met everywhere who questioned her. Admirably loyal, she limited herself to providing meals and lodging, talking about the weather and serving up quite a bit of whisky. This episode must have cost her a fortune in "Canadian Club," but their friendship weathered even this financial drain.

When it was all over, she gave Elizabeth a plane ticket to Florida and the key to the timeshare condominium she and her husband owned in Fort Lauderdale. While Elizabeth tried to collect herself in the Florida sun, Julienne went to see old Mr. Talleyrand, Gérard's boss, without her husband's knowledge, and asked him to give Elizabeth work.

Hubert Talleyrand had always been a lady's man, and felt considerable indulgence toward women who had been seduced. Like many authoritarian men, he also liked to impose arbitrary decisions on those around him; even the most hardened capitalists are, after all, capable of doing a good deed. He was touched by this woman who pleaded in favour of her friend. So he found Elizabeth a discreet little job in inventory. Gérard was not at all thrilled, but he came round when Elizabeth proved herself to be a perfect employee, hardworking, discreet, undemanding, unencumbered by responsibilities such as a husband and children that lower employee output. After some time, he even persuaded himself that he was responsible for getting her started.

If Gérard sometimes liked to recall his generosity, Julienne and Elizabeth hardly ever discussed this sordid subject, or only referred to it indirectly. To give Elizabeth her due, it must be said that she always recognized her debt to Julienne and vowed to return the favour, should some misfortune ever befall her.

Once or twice a week, Elizabeth would stop by Julienne's place after work, while Gérard was off at some "Happy Hour" that he claimed was part of his professional responsibilities. They would have an apéritif together in the kitchen, just the girls.

— I really wish Gérard would get home when you do! Lately it's been worse than ever. He's never home.

— *Naahh!* What would you do with him while you're finishing preparing dinner? Anyway, people in sales always have to socialize.

— *Yesss*, said Julienne in a low, uncertain voice... And she lifted her eyes upwards, which everyone knows is a way of preventing tears from running down your cheeks.

— But it's true that lately it's worse, with the Desourcy account, said Elizabeth with calculated nonchalance. It won't last forever.

— Yes, you're right, answered Julienne in the same low voice.

Elizabeth looked with dismay at her friend's long, pale face. Like the heroine of a popular romance, Julienne was sentimental, loyal and passionate. Unfortunately, she did not have the figure to go with it. Did she know, with the terrible awareness of plain-looking women, that this time something really was going on? The problem occupying Gérard's attention was not the

Desourcy account, but one Blondine Guichard, who worked in promotion, a twenty-eight-year-old Miss Montreal type, competent and well paid. You couldn't even accuse that louse Gérard of harassing some poor underpaid secretary.

Damn him!

In spite of her indignation, Elizabeth proceeded carefully. She mulled over what she knew about the protagonists, their personalities, lives and the link between them. She made sure Julienne had never met Blondine, or vice versa. She found out easily when and where Gérard was meeting his sweetheart.

The Marquis affair had cast a pall over her relationships with men, her life was so dreary... For the first time in a great while, she felt joyful at the idea of hatching a plot. Soon after, Ms. Guichard found a paper neatly folded in four in her mailbox, with one word written on it: "Bitch."

She found the same word, written in red lipstick, on her car windshield: "Bitch." Then, under the door, in her mail, in the garbage, in the glove compartment or trunk of her car, written in chalk in her condominium parking lot of and even, one awful morning, she saw two-metre-high graffiti on the wall facing her ground-floor kitchen window: "Bitch." No more, no less, no threats, not even a bit of slander. Blondine had never been afraid of making enemies; she was driven when it came to her career and determined her self-worth by how much envy she could inspire in others. But when she realized that she never got these messages at Talleyrand and Associates, her suspicions became more specific...

Finally, Elizabeth saw her at the company cafeteria, drinking a very acrimonious cup of coffee with Gérard. Blondine was gesticulating, hissing like a venomous snake, Gérard was looking at the tips of his shoes. Elizabeth decided the moment had come to attack.

One night when Blondine was coming home very late, she was accosted in the underground garage by an unknown woman with colour-damaged hair, orange foundation, dark glasses, a large chest beneath a shapeless raincoat, wearing sweat pants and Adidas.

Some people really know how to make themselves look worse than they already do, Blondine thought mechanically. The woman came out from behind a post at the moment Blondine was closing the door.

— I need to talk to you, said the woman. Her voice was high-pitched, uneven.

— Now? said Blondine with a sigh. You are... ?

— Madame Dubuc. And I'm here to tell you to leave my husband alone!

Blondine inhaled deeply. But before she could say a word, the woman grabbed her raincoat from behind and shook her violently, repeating hysterically:

— Leave him alone! Leave him the hell alone or I'll kill you!

As Blondine was trying to free herself, the woman slapped her violently a couple of times. Blondine hit the wall, landing on her hands and knees on the pavement.

Her cheeks were burning and her pantyhose torn; she heard the other woman running away and a car starting.

Julienne and her husband were peacefully watching a mini-series on television when the telephone rang. Thankfully, the children were already in bed. As soon as Gérard answered, a furious woman's voice let loose a confused flood of curses. As far as Julienne could make out, she was talking about herself, a parking lot and a few slaps; all of this was interspersed with a flood of insults. Her husband, as taken aback as herself, held the receiver at arm's length, as if afraid of being bitten. However, he was not a man to lose composure. When the speaker stopped to take a breath, he took advantage of the moment to hold forth in his most authoritative voice, perfect for chairing meetings and subduing recalcitrant clients.

— Ms. Guichard! I'll have you know that my wife has been here with me since six o'clock this evening! Here, you understand, not in some godforsaken parking lot. I've been patient with you, too patient! But that's it, we'll settle this affair first thing tomorrow! Goodbye!

And he hung up.

Than he went to sit with his wife, who looked at him in shock.

— Julienne, I have something to tell you.

He then told her how Blondine Guichard had been pursuing him relentlessly for months.

— At first I was flattered, I admit, but when she began

telling everyone we were seeing each other and that I was going to marry her, I didn't know what to do. It always looks ridiculous when a man complains about harassment! And normally bosses harass their employees, not the other way around. I had hoped that she'd get over it, but it's gone too far, imagine: this crazy woman thinks you attacked her in her condominium parking lot and uttered death threats! It's one thing for her to plague me all day long, but I won't let her start in on you!

Julienne mumbled: "yes dear, yes Gérard," wringing her hands. Tears of relief welled in her eyes. She could sense he was at least partly lying, and thought confusedly that Elizabeth (who else?) must have something to do with all of this, but tonight, anyway, she would rather hear a few kind lies than the truth.

The next day, Gérard went to see Hubert Talleyrand and spoke to him "like to a father," to use his own expression. And Blondine Guichard was told to take her competencies elsewhere.

Soon afterwards, Elizabeth met Jean-Louis Desjardins, an engineer with Paulin & Lupin. The feeling of having done her duty, even in secret, helped her make peace with herself. She decided that she had paid her dues, and her past no longer weighed her down. Suddenly she opened up for a moment and told Jean-Louis of her past misfortunes. He listened, commiserating.

He himself had been the hero, if it can be called that, of a particularly bizarre divorce. His wife had left him and gone off on a crusade with his car, his savings and a guy she believed would save the world. In doing so, she indebted him throughout America and made a complete fool of him before the entire province. Together they decided to put the past behind them, and that it was never too late to start life over.

Julienne and Gérard were the first to know. After the usual jokes about women who know how to find a good match, Gérard offered to organize a reception in celebration. It was a huge success: people ate, drank and laughed. Gérard knew how to entertain and put people at ease.

While pouring another round of champagne, Gérard told himself that, now that she was getting married, Elizabeth would no longer always be holed up at their place. He begrudged her nothing, of course, but now that he had become once again kindly disposed to family life, it bothered him a little to find her drinking an aperitif in his kitchen every evening.

With the University Set

The intellect is characterized by a natural inability to comprehend life.

HENRI BERGSON, *Creative Evolution*

At the age of forty, Raymond Demers, doctor of mathematics and professor at Université Montmorency, married Céline Dubeau, a cabaret dancer. She was pregnant, and Demers did not want to abandon a child he was sure was his. His colleagues were only moderately surprised by this affair: Demers had always had a reputation for eccentricity. The more embittered ones said he was doing it on purpose to further develop his reputation as a scholar.

For Céline Dubeau, the marriage was unhoped for. Yet she hesitated, out of honesty. She was fourteen years younger than Raymond, and the difference in their backgrounds scared her. Then she looked back over her wandering, solitary life: the sordid hotels, the drunken propositions by men... and accepted. The child, a girl, was born six months after they married. Céline, who came from a background where women's inferiority is taken for granted, was afraid her husband would be disappointed. But Raymond seemed perfectly content, thanked her effusively and gave her a diamond. The truth was that, like many domineering men, he really didn't want a son. And besides, how could a child of his be inferior to anyone? He decided to name her Clara. She was baptized in the Catholic church. Even though he was a notorious free thinker, Professor Demers believed that without Catholicism it was impossible to understand anything about western civilization and its values.

All of this prompted Céline to consolidate her position. She began to observe very seriously the laws and mores of university life. She took courses, read books and knew when to keep her mouth shut. She was astute, and in little time managed to create a character completely in keeping with the wife of a brilliant scientist. Not everything about this undertaking was false or forced; Céline had a few unexpected satisfactions in her quest for bourgeois recognition. The best of these was discovering classical music. When Raymond brought her to hear Beethoven's *Ninth Symphony*, she experienced a violent shock, a kind of revelation. She cried on the way home from the theatre and tried to explain to her husband that "it was too beautiful."

He listened to her pensively and gave her a subscription to the symphony.

As the years passed, Clara grew in beauty. It soon became apparent that she took after her father a great deal, intellectually. It gave him intense satisfaction.

Raymond Demers came from a working-class family: father and sons had worked in the Trois Rivières pulp and paper mill. In this setting, where the ultimate joys were a day off or a case of beer, Raymond had had a difficult childhood and was completely misunderstood. But when he started secondary school with the Marists, destiny placed him in the class of Léon Dubé, a weary, smiling brother who devoted himself to mathematics in order to put some distance between this miserable world and himself. For the first time, Raymond could put a name to the strange passion that tormented him. All at once, his vision changed and he felt singularly in control of the world around him. Now he knew what he wanted. He would be a scientist.

Clara encountered no such obstacles. While still a small child, she walked along the seashore, holding her father's hand while he spoke to her of the unchanging principles that governed the movement of the planets, of this mysterious force, chaos, that defined the shape of the shorelines and the storm systems...

At the age of three, Clara explained to her mother that "zero is different." Céline was worried, and for good reason... Yet in Clara's teenage years mother and daughter became closer. Céline possessed the requisite feminine virtues of compassion, flirtatiousness and acceptance. She was the type of woman who knows how to dress and feeds the birds in winter. Mathematics alone cannot explain the mysteries of life. So Clara's mother told her the facts of life, particularly about relations between people of the opposite sex, and the role of money in the world. They spent delicious, decadent afternoons buying dresses or gorging themselves on pastries. Life is very unfair for girls who are ugly, and Céline did not want her daughter to face the world armed only with her intelligence, no matter what Raymond said.

Clara entered the Faculty of mathematics right on schedule, and distinguished herself, as expected. Raymond stood on the sidelines, ready to intervene without the least compunction, but he didn't have to. Clara did her Master's in the United States and returned to Montmorency for her doctorate.

So what story can be told about so perfect a woman, with so many successes to her credit? It involves men of course... it was to be expected.

At this time, Clara was going out with Jerome Gingras, a young and charming go-getter. Gingras, who was doing a doctorate in civil engineering, was pleasant enough to look at and quite capable, even though he was convinced that the most cynical underhanded manoeuvres were the basic requirements for all success. This observation was not completely unfounded, especially in the university setting, but it was also proof of a limited and rather mercenary mind. At any rate, this sociable and helpful young man was successful in gaining Clara's affection and was tolerated by Raymond, whose feelings regarding any potential son-in-law were very primitive. Intellectually, however, he conceded that a married woman was better off than an old maid, because, even among intellectuals, old-fashioned prejudices prevail. As a result, he welcomed Jerome's obvious allusions to young and brilliant engineers who need help getting their careers started. Some things must be done, and Raymond didn't think that influence-peddling was beneath his dignity.

And Clara? What did she think? Did she find either her father's cynicism or her fiance's unscrupulous ambition despicable? Did she even notice them? Truth be told, it really didn't matter to her. Nepotism was as much a part of her life as snow in January; she was not shocked, having never suffered its consequences. A deeper analysis of the facts would probably have forced her to acknowledge that certain people succeed on their own merit and others need connections. Very likely, Jerome belonged to the second category. But while the world accepts an intelligent man going out with an imbecile, an intelligent woman is expected to find a husband who is at least her equal and who can act as a guarantee, socially. Although convention was not terribly important to Clara, she did not want to be a freak. She therefore studiously ignored all signs of her fiance's lack of character.

One day, in April, Jerome phoned her to tell her that Nelson Larocque, a childhood friend, now a mining prospector in the Northwest Territories, was passing through Montreal. He suggested they all go out together.

They met downtown at a café with an outdoor terrace.

Nelson was a little late. He arrived, moving through the crowd with his long loping stride. He was a tall, slim, muscular man, with a nice smile. Clara found him very good-looking and returned his smile. He gave Jerome a few resounding slaps across the back, showing he was happy to see him, and sat down.

— So you're Clara!

Then, turning toward his friend:

— But she's far too beautiful for you! Aren't you afraid of introducing us? I've just gotten out of the woods!

— But you're going back soon

— I'll risk it.

— How long are you staying in Montreal, Nelson?

— Two weeks. Afterwards, I head for northern Manitoba.

She asked him a few questions about life as a prospector. He answered good-naturedly, as a man who likes his work. Then, he began telling anecdotes, such as how, last fall, he had almost died of starvation during an expedition on the Stewart River.

It was a tale straight out of Jack London, full of endless forests, lost rivers, mysterious mineral deposits and blizzards in September. Packs of lemmings ran beneath the northern lights. Modern times were present in the form of missing air planes, broken down radios and unusable equipment. Nelson told all of this with humour, as if all these tribulations were the reason he had actually become a prospector. Clara listened, laughing until she almost cried, and Jerome looked indulgent, and perhaps a bit annoyed

He and Nelson had known each other as children, and a childhood friendship exerts a strange kind of tyranny... Nelson was stronger, but Jerome was smarter. Jerome was on his way to a successful academic career, and Nelson had left for the Far North after botching acourse in mining engineering. They didn't have much in common anymore, yet there was still a bond between them, the way there is with family.

The three of them often went out to plays, movies or museums. One night, quite late, they went to a discotheque. Nelson asked Clara to dance. And, amidst the darkness and noise, with her head on Nelson's shoulder, she felt a wave of dizziness, and it seemed to her the most natural thing in the world place her mouth on her partner's neck, breathing in the reassuring scent of his skin. He held her tightly, for a long time, then kissed her, eyes closed, as if she were a stranger.

Returning to their table, they spoke of inconsequential things.

Clara managed to be on her own for the next two days. She did nothing special, just loafed around her Nun's Island apartment, looking vaguely at the scenery, the walls, the calendar. The second day she phoned Nelson and suggested they go out downtown.

Jerome was teaching a course that evening. But when Nelson met her, she claimed something unexpected had come up for Jerome. They ate together, then walked around downtown, taking their time. At the end of the evening, Nelson brought her home. They gazed at the city lights from her apartment balcony. Then, calmly, as if she thought the requisite preliminaries had been taken care of, Clara turned to her companion, put her arm around him, and kissed him.

Like many seductive men, Nelson was not really aware of the effect he had on women. He thought quite simply that they were creatures very much ruled by their emotions and their sensuality. In critical situations he preferred them to make very obvious advances to him, to avoid misunderstandings. Once this stage had been reached, he decided that, as the man, it was up to him to take the initiative. He returned Clara's kiss. Then he took her in his arms and carried her into the bedroom.

He awoke early. Clara was sleeping peacefully in the large, rumpled bed. Her body was like a sinuous series of hills beneath the blue sheets. In the kitchen Nelson made coffee and drank a cup, watching the hazy sky. Fleetingly he tried, in vain, to feel some embarrassment or remorse.

— She loves me, he thought to himself. She loves me and, what's more, she's beautiful. He poured a second cup of coffee, to bring to Clara.

He stayed with her until his departure, the next day.

A few weeks later, a delay forced him to spend a week in Thompson, before heading out to the territory he was prospecting. He thought of Clara more than he would have liked, and the small mining town with its prefab houses and its sheds hemmed in by the dark northern forest depressed him. He suddenly decided to go to Montreal for a day or two to see if Clara missed him. He took the first flight and phoned Clara from the Winnipeg airport. She met him at Dorval, calm and cheerful-looking; she didn't tell him she had been afraid he would disappear from her life as abruptly as he had entered it.

And that is how Jerome came to surprise them together on Clara's balcony, on a day on which, more or less by coincidence, he had gone biking on Nun's Island. Clara had told him she intended to break up as soon as Nelson left, but didn't mention Nelson's name, out of a sense of propriety, but also out of superstition. With the annoyed manner of someone being bothered by a door-to-door salesman, she listened to Jerome plead his case and furiously demand explanations. Since then she had ignored him, as if she'd never known him.

Jerome remained at the edge of the bike path for a moment, looking at them, then left, full of conflicting feelings. He had thought he'd stop by Clara's. But he'd always had a keen sense of dignity, and found it inappropriate to stage a confrontation dressed in cycling gear. Besides, Nelson was such a boor he could just as easily have thrown him out the window as offer him a cup of coffee. Thinking it over, Jerome convinced himself that Clara was certainly more to blame than Nelson.

Daddy's little girl thought she was at the centre of the universe and got whatever she wanted. Nelson, would probably have held back due to a primitive sense of friendship, but not to the point of resisting a woman who threw herself at him. Slut!

Nelson returned to Manitoba the next day. Two days later, Jerome went to the faculty of mathematics, where he found Clara in her office. He entered and closed the door behind him. She looked at him without speaking.

— I saw you with Nelson.

— Yes, Nelson...

She uttered her lover's name so happily, so softly, that suddenly Jerome exploded.

— Bitch! Slut! Making a fool of me with a lumberjack!

He slapped her hard. She got up, staggering, to escape him. But he followed her round the room, hitting her again, blocking her way by knocking over furniture and files with savage, unexpected joy. He had planned a very noble scene, complete with reproaches, but it was much more gratifying to beat this bitch up than to argue *ad nauseam* about the nature of love. As he prepared to hit her again, she dodged, ducked under his arm and ran shrieking into the hallway.

It was a terrible scandal. People came to intervene. Jerome escaped those who tried to overpower him and disappeared, running. Clara was crying, shuddering with rage and humiliation. Professor Demers appeared, roaring like a tiger, even more furious when he realized that the infamous aggressor had escaped him.

He brought his daughter home. He seemed calmer when one of his colleagues came for news, and declared very nobly that he would leave the matter in the hands of the disciplinary committee. However, those who knew him were not taken in by this declaration. Behind this magnanimous facade, the beast was sharpening its claws impatiently, and would only be satisfied when Jerome Gingras was reduced to picking through garbage in Timbuktu.

Clara stayed on at her parents and told them the whole story. Her mother took it calmly and remarked simply that she would have been better off laying her cards on the table. Clara blushed and did not answer. Céline tried to contact her daughter's lover, to tell him about what had happened, but he had already left for the taiga. When he returned two months later, he discovered that he had been the hero of a news story.

Raymond was a good deal more perturbed than his wife. Later, when they were alone, he tentatively asked his daughter what Nelson meant to her. He was afraid of a stormy outburst from Clara, whose life he had orga-nized so well. Instead he met with calm certainty.

— Nelson? I love him, Dad. I want to marry him. I love him.

— Yes, of course... but he's someone... whose life is very different from our own, from yours...

She looked at him seriously.

— When you married Mom, it was the same thing. But it worked. You were happy, right? And I don't think I'm all that degenerate!

Her voice trembled slightly. But Raymond had long

known that with Clara, outward signs of emotion were symptomatic of strong resolution.

— Yes, you're right, sorry, I'm just upset.

He stood and looked outside. Clara was twenty-six, old enough to hear some truths. Yet in some circumstances he felt intimidated, as if she were a little girl convinced that her father and mother were holding the dangerous world above her head. His marriage had been happy, certainly, happier than he deserved, but he knew very well that he hadn't married Céline out of love. Love had come later, when he understood that Céline was a worthier human being than himself and because she had given him Clara, the only person to resemble him. Indeed, it was this similarity that disturbed him. Clara was as devoid of altruism as he and committed the same errors in judgment when it came to other people's reactions.

Raymond shared his concerns with Céline. She replied serenely that a man who spent most of his time prospecting in the Far North would certainly suit him better as a son-in-law. As for Jerome, now that his crisis was over, he would calm down and insist that all this be settled in a civilized manner. Being civilized was Jerome's style to a tee; you couldn't say the same thing about the other players in this affair and she hoped that Raymond would have enough good sense not to heap contempt on this unfortunate guy.

The next day, the manager of Clara's building phoned her to tell her that vandals had ransacked her apartment.

The day after, as Clara and Céline were driving home, someone threw a large rock at the windshield as they were going under a small viaduct. The car zigzagged before Céline stopped it on the side of the road. Fortunately, there wasn't any traffic. While Clara remained seated, looking at the star-shaped crack in the glass, Céline got out just in time to see a man, whom she didn't recognize, run away.

They left the car at the closest garage and went home by taxi. There was a message waiting at home. Clara's office at the university had been broken into; there had been an arson attempt. Professor Demers had already phoned the police. No one could locate Jerome Gingras; it seemed he hadn't been home in a day or two.

He had slept on a pallet at the Bonnot shelter, with tramps and drunks. He hadn't changed or washed in three days and was wallowing in morose delight.

He left the shelter at dawn. He bought a can of gas in a 24-hour garage and walked toward the Demers house. All was perfectly calm. He unhurriedly crossed the sprawling lawn. There was a pile of firewood against the wall, where the house met the garage.

Jerome poured gas on the dry wood and then crouched down to strike a match. But his hands were shaking.

— Perhaps you could use some help?

He started violently. He fell seated, the matches scattered around him. Raymond Demers loomed over him, hands in pockets, sneering with contempt.

— You really are an idiot, Jerome. That's the worst thing about you. You're an idiot.

He was going to expound on this subject, but Jerome stood up suddenly and, stammering insults, seized him and began kicking and punching.

— You old bastard! You bastard, you bastard!

Raymond wanted to retaliate, but, suddenly felt an intense pain in his heart and everything started to sway. He didn't fall because Jerome was holding him by his jacket, watching him, dumbstruck. He was still holding him when Céline walked up behind him and hit him on the head with a paddle she had taken from the garage. She made sure she had really knocked him out, then knelt at her husband's side to hold him.

Clara appeared at the kitchen doorway in her nightgown. Her mother yelled at her to dial 911 and bring a bottle of cognac.

The dust finally settled.

Raymond had only had a blackout, a brief loss of consciousness, what the doctors call a heart trouble. He returned home soon after. Jerome had been detained at Parthenais Prison, waiting for the courts to rule on the sorry affair. He found himself in the infirmary, apparently suffering from serious depression. He sent the Demers family a long tearful letter in which he explained in a little less than ten pages that he didn't know what had come over him. It was temporary insanity plus the heartbreak of a failed love affair. He was eternally sorry, and went on and on.

Clara had gone with her mother to Nun's Island to put her apartment back in order. Raymond was therefore alone when the letter came. He read it with disdain and burned it, on the patio. Women were liable to be moved by the most absurd tales, but not him-not a chance. He would make him pay dearly, make that snotty, pathetic degenerate suffer his last breath-that criminal who had proved that he, Raymond, had become an old man.

The Tigress

I could find no other words in which to express my dismay, my alarm and my astonishment at seeing an evil power, whose very name was unknown to my ten years, so transform the gentlest of creatures into a savage brute.

COLETTE, *La Toutouque*

Hélène Tremblay's mother, Léonie Tremblay, had been a pioneer in the world of finance. She had worked as a teller at the Quebec Credit Union before marrying and going to settle with her husband in Lac Saint-Jean. When caring for her progeny-she had six children-left her the time, she realized that the area had absolutely no banking institutions, and she herself had absolutely no occupation outside the house.

She was not a woman to ruminate in vain about a problem. She went to Montreal to meet the board of directors of the Credit Union. At that time, women had just obtained the right to vote. But Léonie, a modern-day Portia, pleaded her cause so eloquently and presented such a heroic portrait of these brave entrepreneurs and farmers, prevented by something as commonplace as a lack of credit from accessing the marvels of the twentieth century. She drew such a flattering portrait of the Credit Union, leader in a dynamic march toward progress, profit and the most patriotic economic expansion-nationalist sentiment was very strong among administrators of the Credit Union-that she received authorization to open a branch where she lived in Sainte-Jeanne-du-Nord. At the outset, this branch depended on the Alma Credit Union. But Léonie proved herself such a shrewd administrator that after only three years she became the first woman bank manager in Quebec. The fact that this was surely the smallest bank in the province didn't change a thing. Later, the Credit Union used her story in its advertisements to show that it had always been an institution ahead of its time.

Hélène was the only daughter in the family. Was she influenced by the example of a remarkable woman? No doubt, for she had inherited from her mother the ability to immediately assess reality and the knack for transforming ideas into actions.

At twenty-one, Hélène decided to found a trucking company. With her savings, augmented by a small loan, she acquired a couple of postal trucks no longer in use, spotted like leopards with anti-rust. She hired two of her cousins as drivers. She drove herself, occasionally, but preferred to limit herself to administrative duties. She transported anything, in all conditions: groceries, hardware, furniture, railway tracks, construction materials, firewood, crews of lumberjacks and even once, a moose captured by the Quebec City zoo.

This last trip became legend. The animal, insufficiently tranquillized, fell into a rage as they were pulling into Tadoussac. It escaped and revolutionized the small city before being captured with the help of the entire local population; alive, and by all accounts quite pleased with itself.

Later, when she lived in Quebec City, Hélène would sometimes see the moose, who appeared to be adapting well to his new life. This animal had become a symbol for her. At the time of its escapade, it could have reduced her to bankruptcy: given the precarious finances of her starting business, she would have been unable to compensate her clients for the loss of the animal. What's more, she liked the fact he had put up a fight.

In the end, this burlesque episode had been excellent publicity. Her business grew. At twenty-eight she had established her base of operations in Quebec City and was the happy owner of a fleet of handsome red trucks, whose emblem was a moose.

She was a beautiful woman, striking, and carried her weight with a great deal of assurance. She decided she hadn't been destined to be thin and that in her profession a little bit of extra weight was an advantage rather than an obstacle.

All the same, she knew how dress in a way that suited her, preferring dresses to slacks, and suede to leather. She had a lovely complexion: rosy, delicate skin with no imperfections, and thick, shiny hair. Her only flaw, physically, was perhaps her eyes: a very pale grey, when she was angry they gave her the implacable look of a statue. She made herself up carefully to minimize this minor imperfection. Her employees had nick-named her "the tigress." She pretended not to know.

Soon after moving to Quebec City, she managed to get on the board of directors of various nonprofit orga-nizations: charitable works, cultural associations and hospitals. She wanted to make contacts, of course, but she also knew that woman cannot live by trucking alone. This is how she met Pierre Renaud, her husband.

She was on the board of directors of the Provincial Association of Professional Musicians. He was a guitar-ist and composer for a group that definitely deserved to be better known. They were introduced at a sympo-sium organized by the PAPM, whose theme was "The Future of Avant-Garde Music in North America."

When she asked him his advice on this far-reaching question, Pierre answered, smiling, that he saw creation as a personal adventure, an act accomplished in soli-tude, and that people who tried to make it a concern of society were just hoping to get some kind of funding. "Music has nothing to do with money, nothing," he added with an even more disarming smile. She agreed dumbfounded; in her experience *everything*, absolutely everything, was linked to money.

The tigress liked men for their looks and their strength. She found ridiculous the traditional idea that men were more suited than she to make decisions and take charge. Nevertheless, she kept this opinion to herself, experience having shown her that men are far too impressionable to face these truths. The only men who truly inspired her had that mysterious, inimitable quality called artistic talent. The phenomenon of creation inspired respect verging on fear; it seemed so inexplicable. And Pierre Renaud was good-looking too, lively and charming, as musicians so often are...

In great agitation, she thought of ways to see him again. There was no need, because a few days later he phoned her to tell her his group would be playing at La Méduse, a coffee house that staged concerts. Would she like to come hear them?

After that, it all went very quickly and they married six months later. Certain spiteful people claimed that Renaud was planning for his old age. In fact, such calculation was completely beyond him. Even though he earned a good living as an arranger and accompanist, he spent money very quickly, and never knew what he'd done with it. Hélène never reproached him in the least on this subject. For her, this insouciance was an integral part of his talent, of all she held dear in him. She simply arranged to manage his contracts and invest his benefits for him.

Pierre Renaud came from the kind of family one reads about in a sociology textbook. His father was a pathetic crook, whose cowardice and laziness were confined to low level fraud, credit card theft, eating in restaurants without paying and passing false cheques. His mother was an accomplice, although she had committed the odd misdemeanour on her own. They had four children, out of simple neglect, both incapable of planning, even when it came to basic aspects of existence. As a result, Pierre, his brother and two sisters passed the greater part of their childhood in poverty and neglect, here and there, spending time in various youth protection institutions.

He was quite relieved, at eighteen, to put all that behind him and pursue his music in peace. He had never found it necessary to discuss his desire to become a musician with anyone. In any case, there was no one to discuss it with. However, it was this ambition that helped him get through his miserable childhood relatively unscathed. The three other children, who had no similar desire shielding them from the bleak corruption of those around them, turned out exactly like their parents, completely justifying the grimmest sociological hypotheses.

When he met his wife, Pierre had long since lost contact with his family. He fell in love because he felt that this woman, like music, was part of his destiny: she was the first human being to give him the assurance of love.

They bought a house in Charlesbourg, had a daughter, Julie, and hoped for at least one other child. Hélène revelled in the most blissful love. Like many tigresses, she was a kindly woman, indulgent even, when her combative instincts were not provoked. Sometimes, when she looked at her child, she thought of the inevitable process that transforms little girls into tigresses and her heart grew heavy. She knew that neither her love nor her money could shield Julie from this. Pierre had no such worries, because he wasn't affected by the ugliness of the world. Had he become immunized from it during his miserable childhood? Hélène didn't know, but she envied him.

One day, going over the balances of various bank accounts, she noticed that Pierre had recently withdrawn considerable amounts from his personal account, at regular intervals. She was overcome with unexplained anguish. Pierre left her in charge of all his accounting, domestic and other. She tried to reassure herself with the idea that he did not necessarily keep her informed of his professional expenses. But a sure instinct was alerted and gave her a premonition of trouble.

Afterwards, it seemed to her the world around her was fraught with danger signs. A mutual acquaintance asked her, feigning innocence, who the girl was that Pierre was dining with the other day. He himself told her about his days in a way that was both evasive and diligent, enough to make the most naive wife suspicious. And the tigress was not naive.

It was the beginning of winter, after the geese had flown but before the snow. They owned a small country house in the area of Cap-Tourmente, but hardly went there this time of year. Getting the phone bill, Hélène was shocked to see that Pierre had made several calls there, from his cellular... First she felt a kind of saddened tenderness; his hopelessness at dissimulating was touching! But at the same time anger, like a storm, welled up inside her.

However, she remained calm. She dialled the number

of the cottage, and when a young woman answered, asked in an even voice to speak to Mr. Renaud. The girl answered acrimoniously that he wasn't there. Hélène insisted, pretending she was calling about property taxes on behalf of the municipality, and that she had to speak to the owner immediately. Would she be talking with Mrs. Renaud?

The girl answered yes, but when Hélène asked if she could stop by city hall, she sensed the unknown woman regretted her unthinking reply. She muttered that Pierre took care of all that and she would let him know when he got in that evening. Hélène reminded her that tomorrow was Saturday and that city hall was only open until noon. She hung up and stared fixedly at the wall.

Pierre had told her that, this weekend, he had registered for a seminar on the new synthesizers or something similar, in Les Éboulements... Nevertheless she remained relatively calm. She phoned the PAPM to verify that her husband had paid his registration fee for the seminar, and found out he had.

Something was definitely going on.

She thought for a moment. Her cleaning woman was tidying the kitchen. She went to find her and explained in a steady voice that something unexpected had come up and she had to go to Montreal. Could Ginette babysit for Julie until tomorrow afternoon?

Ginette assured her she could. Hélène packed a bag, said she would leave from the office without going home and asked her to tell her husband if he phoned. She hugged her daughter devotedly and left. But she didn't go to the office straight away. Her composure was beginning to crack. She knew that she would not be able to control her voice if she spoke to anyone right now.

She went to the zoo, which was open, even though there wasn't much to see at this time of year. The paths were wet and strewn with rotting leaves. The moose was ruminating mournfully at the back of his enclosure. The tigress' heart was brimming over with pain and sorrow, but not a soul knew. It wouldn't last.

When she felt a little better, she went to the office and spent the afternoon inspecting the trucks and chewing everyone out.

She left the office at about four o'clock, to the intense relief of her employees. She took the Quebec City Highway, changing lanes continually, making the transmission screech. The end-of-day traffic distracted her. Yet reaching the road from Beaupré to Saint-Joachim she found it almost deserted; the low, leaden sky of dusk weighed on her chest like a stone.

When she saw a car in front of her house, a sorry-looking Lada, devoured by rust, she sneered ferociously. The proximity of the unknown enemy restored her rich woman's assurance, her tigress' reflexes. She got out of her car slowly and slammed the door deliberately.

She rang and entered. In the dim light of the vestibule, she could make out a woman's silhouette. Turning on the light, she said:

— Madame Renaud? I believe I spoke to you this morning.

She said this in a cordial voice, unfortunately contradicted by a truly cannibalistic smile.

The girl was slim, quite pretty in an anaemic sort of way. She muttered something that the tigress didn't bother listening to. She continued good-naturedly:

— After speaking to you this morning, I thought it would be better if I came because usually, I am Madame Renaud.

She walked into the living room, turned the light on and closed the television. Thus having reclaimed territorial possession, she continued:

— In fact, I think you'd better leave here immediately.

— Pierre gave me permission to stay.

— That may be, but you're still leaving. Immediately.

She accompanied this declaration with a smile worthy of the Kumahum tiger.

— I don't really feel like discussing it, see?

— I'll go when I feel like it, the girl answered stubbornly.

The tigress smiled again.

— You don't understand at all, do you? she said evenly, then went upstairs.

The girl heard the sound of breaking glass, and saw something large and black pass in front of the living room window and plop to the ground. She went outside.

— My suitcase! Are you nuts?

She said no more, because the tigress was busy flinging her clothes out the bedroom window. The ground

was damp and muddy, the girl rushed over to salvage
some items from the disaster. Her arms were full when
Hélène followed her, hands on hips, ordered:

Get the hell out, now!

This time, the girl was angry enough to counter
back:

— A nut! A complete nut! Are you always like this or
is this a crisis? Perhaps you have a gun in the glove
compartment or a bottle of acid in the trunk?

— Listen, girl, said the tigress in a very soft voice, if
you're not happy, go block the Quebec City bridge. Or
call the police if you like. Don't worry, the phone works,
I didn't cut the wires.

This time she saw that she had hit her mark. The
girl's face clouded over with fear. She threw her stuff
into the Lada, cursing unintelligibly, sat in the driver's
seat and drove away without even turning on the lights.

The tigress watched her go, than went back in without
slamming the door. She rummaged in the cabinet and
poured herself a large whiskey, noting with sad indignation that the liquor bottles were almost empty. "A
drunk, too." She fell back on the sofa. Now that her
anger was spent, she was very worried.

She felt even more worried when she heard her
husband's car coming up the hill, half a kilometre
before the house. Still cautious in her love, she invari-
ably recognized the least sign of the loved one. She
heard the car stop and the door slam. She remained

seated. She was shaking, and at that precise moment hated herself intensely.

Pierre entered and remained standing in the doorway.

— So? he said softly.

— Why did you come here? said Hélène in a very low voice.

He looked at her for an instant before replying.

— My sister called me this afternoon. The municipal taxes are in your name, not mine. And I knew that if you'd phoned, you'd be coming here, right? When did you figure it out?

— This morning, going over the accounts. Then brutally: No, it's not true; I didn't understand a thing; not a thing! Why didn't you tell me the truth? Your sister, your sister?

— Listen, Hélène, the police are looking for her, she's been passing bad cheques again. If she gets caught, she'll be charged as a second offender. When she came to see me, she didn't know where to go, had no money and, even temporarily, I knew you wouldn't allow it.

— I couldn't allow it if I didn't know about it! I didn't know she was your sister! I...I...

But this outpouring of sincerity didn't last long. She felt too humiliated! A scene! She had made a jealous scene like some hysterical actress: over him, her sweetheart! And the tigress burst out sobbing, the way a fragile woman does, the way people do on television soap operas. Here husband poured her another whisky. He sat near her and held her close.

— Really, Hélène, really! How could you? Don't you know me better?

— No, I don't know you! When it comes to you I'm blind, I never understand a thing!

She cried again for a bit, uncontrollably, while he waited for it to pass. Finally she asked:

— What'll she do now?

— She'll go to the United States. He shrugged his shoulders. Maybe. In the end, you gave her a good reason for hitting me up for a bundle. She was waiting for me at the bottom of the hill.

— How much?

— Five thousand.

As his wife grimaced, he smiled.

— I know, Hélène, I know. But it really is your fault.

He got up and looked around to assess the ravages of her tantrum. Then he smiled again, as a man who appreciates the trouble someone has gone to for him.

— On top of everything, it seems you threw her suitcase out the window? Couldn't you have opened it first? Not dramatic enough? Did you by any chance think of setting a fire as well? Hélène, Hélène!

Olga

Personally, I have never known a woman really named Olga.

LÉO MALLET, *Le Cinquième Procédé*

Marc André Borduas' first marriage was so disastrous it had become legend.

Among his acquaintances, this topic inspired curiosity that went well beyond mere gossip; people seemed to have a scientific interest in an "interesting case."

They attributed his stubbornness in marrying a girl, half-crazed since childhood, to her dazzling beauty. Many others had been victims of this beauty, but they'd had the good sense not to marry her. When the marriage was announced, Jocelyne Beaudoin's mother had serious pangs of conscience. Shouldn't they tell her fiancé that for years Jocelyne had been cared for by a psychologist, and why?

Mr. Beaudoin fervently dissuaded her. That was all ancient history, the marriage would definitely stabilize Jocelyne. The truth, which he never admitted to anyone but himself, was that he would not let this unheard-of opportunity pass them by: Jocelyne would now be someone else's responsibility. Besides, her therapy had been a huge, useless expense. Jocelyne remained calm for the moment, but her father was certain she hadn't changed.

Her young husband was quite indulgent in accepting the first symptoms of this disorder. Jocelyne spent money extravagantly, and sometimes was overcome by a need to wander the whole day around Montreal, making friends with perfect strangers, and telling childish lies: he found it comforting that his dear little wife needed a man to take care of her.

He changed his mind when he realized Jocelyn was cheating on him right and left, usually with dubious types. Caught in the act, she obstinately and absurdly denied everything. She created melodramatic scenes where, like a heroine in a communist novel, she proclaimed her freedom. Her overriding argument was that she loved him, in spite of his inhuman lack of understanding and petty bourgeois mind set. All of this was uttered in a flood of tears. More than anything else, Marc-André was frightened by this love she brandished like a knife. He asked himself what wrong he'd done to make his wife feel the need to betray and humiliate him.

He showed patience worthy of a better cause. He understood that she was sick and couldn't or didn't want to control herself. At that point he was teaching history and political science at the Cégep du Vieux-Montréal. He forced himself to spend more time with her, sharing his own interests with her. He took her to various political meetings, discussion groups, third world film festivals. Things seemed better for a time, although he found his wife's enthusiasm for any kind of liberation movement dangerously indiscriminate.

One fine day, she disappeared, leaving him a letter on the kitchen table. This missive informed him, in her usual dramatic style, that she had fallen in love with someone named Ramon, with whom she had gone off with to liberate the people of Columbia. No news of her came until later, when she was arrested for an assassination attempt on Judge Miguel Garcia-Gonzalvez, in the company of some Columbian nationals, but without Ramon, who had "miraculously escaped the forces of justice," according to the newspapers. To make matters worse, Marc-André learned that Ramon was no Bolivar, but rather a trafficker "well known to police" and that this affair was further complicated by some dubious blackmail scheme, never brought to light.

In short, Jocelyne was condemned for aiding and abetting. When they told him that, with the usual precautionary measures, Marc-André took it all very calmly. He was relieved, in fact Jocelyne had gone too far this time: he abandoned all responsibility for her. He let a lawyer friend represent him in this affair and obtain his divorce. He requested and was granted a transfer to an outlying area: Trois-Rivières.

Olga Muëller found herself in Trois-Rivières for reasons that were not so very different. A German, she had gotten married very young to a man old enough to be her father, a brilliant academic: inscrutable, manipulative and tormented by a sick taste for schemes of any kind. This seducer, named Andreas, had done with her as he pleased. She freed herself from him only when she realized that he didn't care about their son Hans, who had no place in his father's schemes. A man such as Andreas did not care to be burdened by an old-fashioned, bourgeois sentiment such as paternal love: nobler causes inspired him.

She decided to leave with her child and make a complete break; she emigrated to Canada. At Andreas' instigation, she had studied accounting. Although his suggestion was no doubt motivated by personal interest, in the end it turned out to Olga's advantage. She had no difficulty finding a good job at the National Bank. Given her linguistic competencies, her employers were mildly surprised when she asked to be transferred outside Montreal, but she justified her request by explaining that living in Montreal was like living in Frankfurt, and that wasn't why she had immigrated to Canada.

She was very blond, wide-hipped, soft-spoken and had a peaceful smile. Although not exactly pretty, she had a serenity about her that was pleasing. She coldly assessed her tormented youth and disappointing marriage: what a stupid girl she had been! All she retained was the feeling she had barely escaped serious danger and a conscious taste for happiness.

She met Marc-André at an "open-house" at the Trois-Rivières Cégep. Olga attended these kinds of events so she could meet people and explore the social scene.

Marc-André Borduas owed his excellent professional reputation to his extraordinary eloquence, in which emotion debated with logic. He knew how to convince the dullest class that it *could* and *must* change the world. Strangely, this passionate man was an ardent federalist in a milieu where such political opinions were rare and discreet. Perhaps it was his way of not conforming.

On the day Olga heard him for the first time, he was giving so expert a lecture on "The Founding of Confederation" with so much vigour that his listeners could have believed themselves assembled in Charlotte-town for the founding of a new democracy.

Soon after, she ran into him at the bank. She complimented him on his lecture, and told him she had borrowed a book from the library on Canadian history and asked what "Herr Professor thought of the current situation."

In spite of what had happened in the past, Marc-André was by nature inclined to be happy; he liked summer for the sun, winter for the snow, autumn for the clear blue sky and spring, simply because it was spring. He liked the dark forest of Mauricie because it resembled eternity; he liked the St. Laurence because it resembled life, and the huge cargoes that dominated the port of the small city spoke the promise of dreams beyond measure.

He loved Olga because, while he was crossing the desert, she had already been waiting for him, only for him-even if she didn't know it.

Like many of her compatriots, Olga believed that Latins have a gift for enjoying life. Marc-André's idealism and enthusiasm seemed to her characteristic of this precious trait. Besides, he was a charming husband, attentive and confident. Having Olga's son around did not bother him, quite the opposite. Jocelyne had never shown anything but indifference bordering on hostility towards children. From this point of view, he found Olga's love for her son reassuring.

He gave her a log cabin as a wedding present, set in among the spruce trees, so she could realize her European fantasy of a "cabin in Canada." He also helped Olga obtain the innumerable newspapers, magazines and reports she devoured. She barely read any novels, but voraciously devoured periodicals of all kinds: in German, English, French and Spanish. She read them from beginning to end, including the ads. Her husband joked to her about this; she smiled at him without answering. She loved him madly, with a passion bordering on ferociousness, which her peaceful face never revealed...

They learned in the newspapers that Jocelyne had been liberated for health reasons and that she was returning to her family.

Then the letters started.

They came at irregular intervals, and varied in length; some were written over the course of many days, others on the spur of the moment. Alternately tearful, threatening and angry, all of the letters were incoherent: Jocelyne had not changed. Marc-André was so overwhelmed he couldn't hide them from his wife, as he would have liked. It seemed the past was coming back to haunt him. He was sure of it when Jocelyne began to phone him at all hours of the day and night, write raving missives to his superior and threaten to come explain her side of things; she considered they were still married. Olga took it all calmly. She advised him to reply only once, refuse all contact, and to alert the Beaudoin family as well as his lawyer. The letters stopped and Marc-André told himself that he had worried for nothing. He began to hope that Jocelyne would leave him in peace.

He was wrong. The letters had stopped coming because Olga was intercepting them, answering them herself.

She worked half-time at the bank and the mail was delivered after Marc-André had gone. She had intercepted the first letter simply to spare her husband useless suffering. But her noble intentions were rapidly replaced by cold fury. Olga decided to take matters into her own hands.

The only letter Marc-André sent his ex-wife had been written on a computer, to make it as impersonal as possible. Olga photocopied her husband's signature on blank sheets on which she typed her replies.

She was not afraid of being found out. If his first wife showed up in Trois Rivières to create a scandal, Marc-André would believe that she, Jocelyne, had plotted the whole story, because he of course hadn't written...

Besides, ever since she thought she had recaptured the attention of the man she still considered to be her husband, Jocelyne's letters had become more reasonable, even rather conspiratorial in tone. She gave in quite submissively to Olga's admonition for discretion, "on account of my wife"...

But time passed and Olga could see that she could not maintain the status quo indefinitely. Jocelyne was becoming impatient; she spoke of settling things once and for all, of coming to Trois-Rivières and having it out. Worse still, she suggested a weekend reunion, at the Beaudoin cottage in Rivière-aux-Rats.

Near the end of winter, some favourable circumstances brought about a meeting. Marc-André was supposed to go to a conference on teaching reforms in Quebec City. The same weekend, a neighbour offered to take Hans to the cottage to keep her little boy company. Like all those who love, Olga had a superstitious side. Everything in the universe seemed to conspire: she saw her destiny everywhere, from the stars up above to the bus schedules. Olga declared that she would go to her "cabin in Canada" and make a few repairs. It was time for action.

She sent Jocelyne a very short letter in which "Marc-André" agreed to meet her at the Beaudoin's house in Rivière-aux-Rats. She was sure that the secretive tone of the letter and her heeding for discretion would appeal to Jocelyne. She had a little trouble making her other preparations without changing her family routine, but finally, on the Friday night, she calmly wished both her husband and her son a good trip. The next morning, she left home very early.

She arrived in Rivière-aux-Rats after Jocelyne. As she had noticed during her reconnaissance, the road was well-cleared, even if the house was quite isolated, especially at this time of year. She parked the car carefully, not feeling particularly nervous. When Jocelyne left the house and waited to stare at her, open-mouthed, Olga, standing near the car, smiled kindly at her. She went up to the balcony and said:

— I'm Olga. Shouldn't we go in?

In the living room, Jocelyne stayed near the door for a moment, glancing sideways at the other woman, and said:

— What are you doing here?

— I came here to talk to you. Apparently there are some things you don't understand very well.

She went on:

—I'm the one who arranged this meeting.

She waited to let Jocelyne have time to digest this information. But Jocelyne replied immediately:

—No, it was my husband.

—First of all, he's no longer your husband. You're divorced, and he remarried because you'd gone off with someone else.

Olga said this in the same reasonable tone she would have used in discussion with a bank client.

—I still have all his letters!

—He wrote you once, to tell you to leave him alone. When you kept on writing, I intercepted the letters.

Jocelyne shrugged her shoulders pensively. Perhaps this manoeuvre seemed quite understandable to her. She declared, nevertheless:

—That doesn't change anything. Marc-André has to come back to me.

She added, as an explanation:

—I fought with my family. My father found me an apartment on the Plateau. He pays the rent but forbade me to move back in with them. Marc-André is going to have to do something.

—Why did you fight with your family?

Jocelyne launched into a confused diatribe, listing all the offenses inflicted upon her by her heartless bourgeois family. Olga listened without interrupting; she needed time to think. All this was becoming distressing, as she had feared. When Jocelyne started to philosophize about her family's disgraceful behaviour, Olga rose:

—It's suffocating in here. Perhaps we could go for a short walk?

Jocelyne didn't answer, but put on her coat and they went out onto the large terrace behind the house. The river was visible in the distance, behind the trees. Jocelyne asked:

— What are you going to tell Marc-André?

— Nothing, Olga replied peacefully. He broke off with you. And besides he knows nothing about this. Why would I talk to him about it?

— In that case, *I'll* talk to him.

Olga clenched her fists in the pockets of her jacket, forcing herself not to sigh or roll her eyes. What a stubborn idiot!

— Do you think so? You've always needed to bother someone, whether it was Marc-André or someone else, right? And Ramon? Did you manage to make life impossible for him as well? Perhaps that's the reason he handed you over to the police?

— Ramon?

— Your Ramon-the one who miraculously escaped police. After that ridiculous attempt when they arrested you others so easily. In fact, he framed you, said Olga with her kind smile.

— Ramon joined the guerillas again.

— Did you hear from him when you were in prison? Or since you got out?

— He joined the guerillas again!

— If it's true, why aren't you waiting for this hero, rather than harassing your ex-husband?

Jocelyne didn't answer. She stared stubbornly at the river, at the horizon. She didn't see Olga step backwards, remove a rock that she had slid into a sturdy nylon sock, and steadily swing the improvised sling. She realized something was happening a fraction of a second before being hit in the temple. She fell in a heap. Olga hit her again, carefully, on the same side of the head.

Then she straightened up, and looked around. Good. She left her jacket on the terrace and entered the house, looking for the keys to Jocelyne's car. She picked up Jocelyne's suitcase and closed it. She went out again, put the suitcase in the trunk, opened the door of the passenger side and carried Jocelyne to the car. She returned to get her jacket and locked the house. She started the car, and drove away cautiously, slowly, until the first intersection, where she turned. The road led to an abandoned quarry. Olga parked as close as possible to the edge and got out of the car. She opened the other door and pushed Jocelyne into the driver's seat. She shifted the gear into neutral, then went behind the car and pushed. The car plummeted and was buried in a mass of snow at the bottom of the quarry, making hardly a sound. Olga would have preferred to burn the car, but this was impossible. She returned to the house on foot. The sky was darkening.

She inspected the house, making sure nothing was lying around and wiping clean all surfaces she had touched. She had not found the letters in Jocelyne's things: that would have been too easy. So she would have to go to Montreal. But first she had to retrace her steps, and return to the shopping centre near the entrance to Trois-Rivières to abandon the car she had stolen and take back her own. She did not want to risk driving on the highway in a stolen car.

She arrived in Montreal without a problem. It was already nine o'clock at night and snowing heavily. She left the car near the Crémazie station and took the metro to Mont-Royal. She entered Jocelyne's apartment with the key she had kept, with the benevolent air of someone come to water the plants and pick up the mail. She quickly found the letters, checked the answering machine and hid any evidence of a recent departure. She left, locking the door behind her, and got back on the metro. By eleven o'clock she had reached highway 40. It was snowing more heavily-not a storm, but it took her some time to get back to the "cabin in Canada." No matter. She had no neighbours or telephone there; no one could check what time she had come in. She would begin to put things back in order tomorrow. She sighed like someone who sees the light at the end of the tunnel. For the first time in a long while, she thought without bitterness of her first husband, Andreas. So everything in that absurd and wild escapade had not been in vain—the best part of their marriage had been in the bad old days of the Baader-Moorhoff gang. And besides, wasn't it with Andreas' skin that she had bought this new life for Hans and herself?

The Huntress

And then came what everyone awaited, love on
sparkling golden wings.

ARISTOPHANES, *Birds*

She had seen him at the university-in the classrooms, at the cafeteria. She spent the entire "German Silent Film" seminar contemplating his profile, the shape of his head beneath his closely cropped ash-grey hair, the supple movement of his shoulders inside old sweatshirts.

He was always perfect-even when he was devouring overcooked pasta in the pale cold light of the cafeteria, even when he was bored. She would see him sometimes in the cafés and businesses that spring up automatically around a university.

She spoke to him only once, in the laundromat, where she found him reading a P. D. James novel. As she admired this author a great deal, it gave her the courage to initiate conversation. He told her with the nicest smile that he too liked English detective novels and that his name was Jacques. When his two pairs of jeans and his three shirts had finished spinning in the dryer, he said goodbye with the same dazzling smile.

❧

She danced with him at an evening supposedly orga-
nized for solidarity with Nigerian intellectuals (no
Nigerians were visibly present). He told her he was
happy to see her again and put his arm around her to
lead her to the dance floor. The sensual African music
almost sent her into a trance. When, emboldened by
the blissful darkness, she suggested they go have a
drink, he told her politely that he had a night job and
that he had to leave now. And he did, just like Prince
Charming.

She knew nothing about him.

❧

Sylvie had wanted to become a forestry engineer. Her
mother ridiculed her decision, but in any case her
mother had always looked at whatever she did, indeed
her very existence, most critically. Having become a
widow early on with a young daughter, Madame
Claudette Trépanier fully blamed her for the fact she
couldn't "start over," and went on at great length about
the penance she had endured in the name of maternal
duty. It never occurred to her that her pettiness, her
perpetual recriminations and the sight of a mother incapable of loving her only child were enough to scare off
even the stupidest man.

Sophie chose her profession with the desire to
escape the life of suffering her mother had tried to
impose on her, but was also influenced by long

summers spent in her Uncle Adrien's house in Saint Donat.

Sylvie's father, Daniel Trépanier, and Adrien Cadieux had been childhood friends, which is why Adrien had encouraged Daniel Trépanier to marry his sister. He regretted this as one of the only mistakes of his life. He had thought Daniel's kindness and generosity would rub off on Claudette, a rather colourless creature. On the contrary, the marriage had brought out her worst aspects: selfishness, stinginess and deceitfulness.

Adrien blamed himself that Daniel, whom he had loved so much, and who had died so young, had not been happy, and that his only child was no happier. As a result, he strove to watch over the little girl, and Sylvie could often be found with him and his four children.

This also meant that his sister was around a lot more than he would have liked, but he humbly accepted this. Sylvie grew up alone, yet without too much bitterness. Thanks to Adrien and his family, she knew that there was more to life than empty regret.

The day after the Nigerian evening was a Sunday. A melancholy Sylvie wandered around the Plateau Mont-Royal, cursing her own stupidity. She didn't know how to reach Jacques. They had no friends in common; she didn't even know his last name. Walking in front of Wolfman's fish market, she raised her eyes and stopped suddenly in front of the marvellous graffiti that for a long time graced the parking lot: AMOR OMNIA VINCIT.

She knew a bit of Latin. She walked away slowly, thinking.

The next day she placed the following ad in the "personal" column of various alternative weekly newspapers: "Ever since Nigeria, Sylvie has been seeking Jacques."

She put no phone number or address. She could not allow herself to become distracted from concentrating. She put the same message on the electronic message system at the university, a tiny missive carried along by this flood of information.

She phoned radio programs that took special requests and asked them to play the most idiotic love songs "for Jacques." She wrote their two names on blind walls and construction site fences. She lit votive candles at Notre Dame Church and ventured into the most exotic places of worship in the city, asking priests, who were either welcoming or shocked, for "a small prayer."

She did all of this carefully, patiently, like a weaver hard at work at a complicated design. Concentration and perseverance were important. When she fell short of inspiration, she would begin phoning at random, until she reached an answering machine: "Jacques, please call Sylvie."

Bewitchment is a process involving many unpredictable risks, because it is inextricably linked to the personality of the person casting the spell, the nature of his
request, and casual events. Still, the biggest risk is the
most common: the person who casts the spell actually
becomes bewitched, and is detached from reality in a
way that runs counter to the most basic instincts of
self-preservation. He ends up smashing his face falling
on the sidewalk, becomes a victim of a traffic accident
or the smallest cold develops into pneumonia. He
forgets to go to work, or pay his rent. Moreover, such
long and intense concentration on just one object
makes him extremely vulnerable to the thoughts of his
enemies.

Sylvie was naturally resistant to the effects of
bewitchment, because she was young, sane and solitary,
and, coming from a long line of patient farmers and
resigned workers, in her flowed the blood of ancestors
who had abandoned civilization for the wilderness with
the disconcerting ease of the converted. These people
had discovered their hearts' allegiance in the dark
northern forests and sparkling rivers. And they had
simply forgotten their past. Exiled in the metropolis,
Sylvie continued to read predictions in the colour of
the river and the sound of the wind, she followed the
path of the constellation above the skyscrapers, and
was never afraid at night.

And her dream was as one might expect.

On a spring morning, with the weak sun shining, she crossed the postmodern cemetery that lies beyond the Voyageur bus station. She was thinking about the approaching summer and while she walked she freely bestowed her indifferent smile. It was one of those days where the forces of nature and destiny irrepressibly converge.

Sylvie was dreaming. Marie Island was stretching like a tall, captive animal, and tearing away the iron harness of the bridges and pylons chaining it to the shores of the river; it swam to the sea to join its sisters, l'Isle Verte and Anticosti. This vision filled her heart with savage joy, which is why she only saw Jacques at the last minute.

He broke away from a group of friends and came toward her, guitar in hand. She was coming down the granite steps and the grey stone shone in the new light. She stopped when she heard Jacques call her name. He went up to greet her and stopped one step below. He put his arm around her and said:

— I'm happy to see you. Where were you all winter?
— Here, she replied.
And she kissed him on the lips.